I0550216

Email…

I would love to hear your feedback, email me at
candacy75@hotmail.com

Demons Beware

Dedication:

I would like to thank Anne Dehn for all her help in writing this book. I couldn't have done it without you! I would also like to thank Sue Lavender for editing this book; I know it took a lot of time and hard work. Thank you to my friends and family for always being there for me and telling me I can do anything I put my mind too. Last but not least, thank you to my wonderful daughter, Katlyn, if it wasn't for you, this book wouldn't be possible.

One

"Well Cady, I would probably say you're dreaming," I said to myself. I was standing alone in a field surrounded by the biggest black and pink flowers that I had ever seen, flowing in the breeze. They were a least six feet tall, looking like they were trying to reach up and touch the sky. The trees behind them were tall, and massive. I couldn't see even half the way up the top. It was like looking up at the biggest skyscraper I had ever seen. "Great, I went to sleep and ended up in Giantville, I hope there's a giant chocolate chip cookie somewhere around here. I'm starving," I muttered to myself.

I looked up to see the mountains in the background. I must say it's really beautiful here. I'm standing there looking around. Wondering what kind of dream this is and how in the world I got here. I'm hoping like hell there will be no monsters sneaking up behind me, cause those kind of dreams just suck. As I walked through the field of flowers, the wind picked up and all of a sudden, the wind started blowing harder. Making my hair fly everywhere, whipping in my eyes and around my face.

I hate when I don't have my hair put up in a ponytail, it gets in my face and I can't see anything. Just then Snow started falling around me. I picked up a snowflake, it wasn't cold. It was grey and it looked like ash from a fireplace.

I suddenly heard a noise that sounded like ocean waves crashing over wave after wave and down on rocks, but it had a sizzling noise to it. Almost like the sound of water hitting something very hot, "What the...." was all I could get out. When I looked up and finally got all my hair under control and out of my face, I couldn't believe my eyes. They must be playing tricks on me, I thought. It was like seeing two big, huge, red eyes flying towards me.

I looked closer; well shit not eyes, but two lava rocks shooting through the sky. It was burning everything it touched. A wave of lava headed down the mountain right towards me. The trees weren't slowing it down. In fact when the lava hit the trees, the branches burst into flames and the leaves went flying everywhere. It looked like a wild woman on crack; "Oh crap!" was all I could think to say. I started to turn around to run the other way, and I will be damned if it wasn't behind me too. I was surrounded by lava!

The flowers started melting and welting around me. "Ok, Cady, you're a witch, they say the most powerful witch anyone has ever seen. I'm a smart girl, surly I can think of something to do to get out of this crap." Ok, its lava, and very hot, so.... I'll freeze it! I centered myself, started concentrating and took a deep breath held my arm up and palm out. Nothing happened, I waited and tried again, but again nothing happened. Well shit!

"You've got to be freaking kidding me! This better be a damn dream! I can wake up any second now!" I yelled in the air, hoping my sleeping body would somehow listen to me. The lava was getting closer and hotter. I could feel the heat touch my face. When I looked down my shoes were starting to melt into the earth. "Come on, Cady, wake up!" I cried.

I looked up to the sky just in time to see someone, or should I say some shirtless guy, either jumping or falling out of the sky. Either way he looked damn good doing it. He landed right in front of me. Before I could look up to see his face, he bent his head down to my neck and wrapped his arms around my waist.

"Hold on tight." he whispers. He doesn't have to tell me twice. Any hot guy that tells me to touch him, I'm all for it. I reached up, put my arms around his neck and held on tight. Mmm, and what a nice strong neck it is. I put my

head in the crest of his neck and looked down to his chest. What I could see was beautiful.

He had a nice golden tan and a six pack to die for. My mouth started watering just thinking about what I could lick off those abs, whip cream and chocolate came to mind. Staring at his chest I saw a tattoo of something, but I couldn't see it clearly. I forgot all about the lava, until I looked further down and seen the earth.

It was a good fifty feet below us and we were falling back down fast! I wrapped my arms tighter around his neck, closed my eyes and hung on for dare life. "Oh shit!" I yelled. It seemed that was the only two words that I could come up in this dream.

He chuckled, "Don't look down, and just keep your eyes closed."

What the hell was I thinking? Who is this guy? Hell, could I even trust this guy? Sure he had a great body and he did kind of save me from the lava, but still we were falling and then going back up. That didn't make any sense to me at all. I felt us coming back down again, but this time I didn't feel us going back up. I could still feel the heat of the lava coming closer, but I wasn't afraid. He kept his arms wrapped around my waist.

I opened my eyes to see darkness with a tad bit of light beaming around the trees. I still couldn't see his face, only a dark shadow around the most amazing emerald green eyes that I have ever seen! It was like they were almost glowing. I couldn't tear myself away from staring at them. I felt like a fat man with his hands around a mouth-watering, juicy steak. He bent down where I could see his prefect plump lips inch their way to mine. They were mere inches away. He brushed his lips to mine and whispered "I'm so sorry." I think I quit breathing for a minute. I was so caught up in his eyes and how close his lips were to mine.

I stumbled "What..... Where are we? Are we going to die?" He didn't move, didn't take his arms from my waist.

His lips brushed mine again. "I'll always be here with you. I love you Catalina, no matter what happens. I'll never leave you."

The heat from the lava was getting worse. I felt like I was starting to melt, or burst into flames. He looked around like he was nervous about something. When he looked again, his eyes were full of concern. "You have to wake up now!" He demanded.

I sat straight up in bed and looked around, he was gone. I tried to get my breathing under control and relax. I looked around my room; I didn't see anything out of place. My clothes that I wore the night before, was still in a pile in the corner where I threw them. The clock on my nightstand said 3:15am. I looked over to the window, which was slightly open so the cool autumn breeze could blow in.

Was it just a dream? It felt so real, his touch, his smell and his hard body. I lay back down on my pillow, trying to fall back asleep again. I was thinking about his eyes and how it felt like they could see deep into my soul. "Damn, it was just a dream. Well that just sucks." I muttered to myself as I fell back to sleep.

Two

I woke up a few hours later, lying in bed still smiling about my hot dream guy. I finally rolled out of bed to get ready for school. I jumped in the shower and just stood there letting the warm water flow over me relaxing all my tense muscles. I could stay in here forever, well, until the water started turning cold.

I decided then that it was time to get out and get ready for the day. I put on a pair of my faded, torn blue jeans and red t-shirt that hugged my body and shows all the right curves. My C cups now looked like D cups. I threw on my work boots and called myself ready. That's my wardrobe. I don't like getting all dolled up, you never know whose ass you might have to kick. I don't care who are, you can't be kicking ass in high heels. Well, unless you're a porn star I'm sure they're used to the heels, but not me.

I went to the mirror to put on my make up for the day and noticed my eyes right off. They were always a little different. I have teal eyes with specks of blue and gold in them. But, now the gold specks were now streaks, making me think of lightning bolts.

"This is different; I hope I don't have to wear contacts to cover these babies up. Oh well….. Happy birthday to me." I laughed. When I was completely done with my clothes and make up, I went to the floor mirror to check myself out. I didn't look too bad if I do say so myself. I'm 5'4 with a long slim toned body. It better be toned anyway, since I work my butt off every day with kickboxing and running two miles. I have long blond hair with natural red streaks that comes to middle of my back. I don't have that nice golden skin you see in magazines. It's white, plain, not pasty white, but just fair. I try and stay out of the sun as much as possible. I get burned too easy and that just hurts. But, overall I guess I'm decent enough looking.

My phone started buzzing "Burn it to the ground" by **Nickelback** and I knew who it was without looking. Bani, my best friend since we were two, she's also a witch, "Hey Bani, what's up?"

She started singing, "Happy birthday toooo yoouuuu!" She sang loudly. "How's it feel to be eighteen? "Just think today you get all your powers in full swing…well tonight anyway" she said loudly.

Being a witch you get half your powers at thirteen and the rest at eighteen. I guess the great ones above didn't think you could handle them all at once. When I turned thirteen and started using my powers, no one could understand why I was so powerful at such a young age. I was doing what most did at eighteen already.

My mom said it was because I was special. I know, what mom doesn't say their kid is special, right? She said it was because I was born on October 13th at 1313 military time, in room 13. So on my thirtieth birthday it was thought that I'd become some great and powerful witch.

Well, if I was so powerful I should be more like Bani. She is a month older than me, and already has her full powers. Her main power is air; she can bring the wind to speeds up to an F-5 tornado. She hasn't tested to that limit yet. The last time she tried to use her wind power, she blew down a barn. She said wind is hard to control, but if she had to, she could destroy cities.

She has long, curly blue-black hair with a bounce in it. She's very pretty with grey eyes that shine. Bani wears all black for some reason, but it fits her. She's the Barbie doll Goth girl. She's 5'6, not a short 5'4 like me. She can talk to anyone that she comes across. I don't think that girl ever met a stranger in her life. I am totally opposite in comparison to her.

I never felt like a powerful anything. I'm just me trying to get through life like everyone else. Sometimes I think it should have been Bani, who was supposedly more powerful.

"Hey, Cady, you still there?" Bani yelled in the phone. That brought me back from day dreaming.

"Oh sorry. Yeah it's ok, I really don't feel any different though. Well except for my eyes that is. They're a little different," I said.

"Really? Their amazing looking already so how could they be different. Let me guess mmm….they're normal now?" she said laughing.

"No, and don't be an ass," I laughed. "You know the gold specks in my eyes?" I said.

"Yeah, why?" she asked.

"Well now I got gold streaks instead. My eyes look like they have lightning bolts in them now. I don't know….. They just look weird to me. What if people make fun of me?" I guess she was thinking about it for a minute before she answered.

"I'm sure they still rock. It'll just take you some time to get used to them, that's all." And that's why she was my best friend; she always saw the brighter side of things no matter what.

"Yeah, maybe. Hey, are you almost here?" I said changing the subject.

"Yup, be there in about five minutes. You do have breakfast ready for me, right?" she snickers. She knows how much I hate cooking.

"Umm, no, it's my birthday, but while you're cooking I'll tell you about my dream I had last night. It was really weird, but really good too." I knew she couldn't resist.

"Please tell me it was a good old fashioned wet dream!" she pleaded.

"You're such a perv! But it was good." I laughed.

Bani replied, "OK, pulling in now. Oh and Cady, if I have to cook…. It better be a good one!"

Bani walked in the door a few minutes later. I was walking down the stairs to meet her. She looked up from digging in her bag for heaven knows what.

"Oh my heaven sake your eyes they…..they do rock! They look freaking amazing!" she said with her hands flying everywhere. I swear she talks more with her hands then her mouth.

"Really? They look ok then…not to weird?" I asked. She just looked at me like I was the one who was nuts.

"Are you kidding me? I'm telling you they rock. You'll drive all the men hard with those babies." She giggles. I just shook my head, rolling my eyes, and walked past her laughing.

"You're such a freaking perv. Are you gonna make me breakfast or just let me starve?"

We headed into the kitchen. She was getting the bacon and eggs out when she stopped and stared at me. "Well, you gonna tell me about this great dream of yours? Or just make me suffer longer?" she asked.

"Oh I think I'll let you suffer. That's always so much more fun." I said with a wink.

"You're such an ass sometimes, Cady." She said laughing as she went to turn on the stove to start breakfast.

We sat down at the table eating when I finally spoke up. "It was the most amazing and horrible dream rolled in one. First, there were these flowers and then lava. Then out of the blue this hot guy jumps out of the sky and saves me."

She lifted her brow. "Ok skip the almost dying crap and go straight to the hot guy. What'd he look like? How'd he smell? How big was he? And I'm not talking body size either, but I do want to know that too. What color......?"

I held up my hand. "OK, ok will you slow down? You're asking way too many questions and there're all running together. I can't keep up. First question, yes he was hot, from what I could see anyway. He had the brightest emerald green eyes that I ever seen. He smelled like the ocean breeze on a summer night with a hint of aftershave. He had a six pack of hard abs with some kind of tattoo on his chest. The women from the old days could do their washing on those abs and love every minute of it. As for how big he was in other places. I don't know, but I would've loved to find out!" I laughed. "For some reason it seemed like he knew me. I don't know how to explain it."

Bani put her hands on the table and looked at me. "Ok, so let me get this straight in my head. You had a dream of a hot guy that seemed to really like you and probably wanted you, but you didn't make a move? Is that about the gist of it?"

I thought for a second before I answered, "Well, yeah, I guess that would be it."

Bani started laughing as she said, "Awe Cady, that's not a dream! That's your real life, babygirl! Guys would cut their right leg off to be with you and you just blow them off like you don't have a clue."

"I do not blow them off! I've dated and what happen when I did? Well let me remind you. The half-demon psycho tried to burn my car up with me in it! So I'm fine with not dating right now! Thank you very much!" I was just getting pissed at this point. I could feel a tingle in my eyes.

Bani had a look on her face that I don't think I ever seen before... horror. She was scared, but she was also looking at me. "Bani, why the hell are you looking at me like that for?" I snapped. Then seeing her scared like that I felt kind of bad. "Crap, Bani," I said going to her side. "I'm sorry…I wasn't yelling at you. I was yelling more at myself."

Bani blinked a few times, before she finally spoke up and it was more of a whisper. "Cady, your eyes just turned completely gold. I couldn't see any other color in your eyes…….What the hell was that about?"

"I don't know. I felt kinda pissed off, because you always make fun of me about not dating." I sat back in my chair and thought about it. I couldn't think of anything that would have made my eyes change like that. "Maybe it's part of my full powers coming into play." I shrugged, "We really didn't know what would happen when I turned eighteen."

Bani thought about it and came to the same conclusion. "Yeah, you might be right. Just try not to get pissed off again ok? That crap was….was weird and freaking scary," she said. Bani came over and put her hand on mine, "I'm sorry for making fun of you. You know I don't mean it."

I smiled, "I know, and I'm sorry for freakin you out. I didn't know my eyes could do that."

Bani stood up and looked down at me, "But, really don't do that shit again."

I laughed putting my hand over my heart. "Ok, I'll try my best."

This time Bani laughed, "Well let's hope so. Now time for your birthday party! We're going out to a club tonight!" She was jumping up and down, "We even have Zane going with us!"

I looked at her like she was the one crazy this time. "Let me get this right….we're going to go to Willey's, to make total fools of ourselves. Then wake tomorrow morning for work and have to see those same people from the club walk into Elementz? How in the world will anyone take us serious again?"

Elementz is a little crystal shop Bani and I work at. Willey's is the town twenty-one and under club everyone goes too. It's not a very big town so everyone knows everything that goes on.

"Oh Cady, chill It will be fine, besides we're not going to Willey's tonight. We're going to the big night club in….. Wait for it….. Wait for it…..Jaggers in Kansas City! How's that sound?" She said throwing her hands up in the air.

I just smiled, "Great. That sounds great, Bani. I can't wait to see what happens tonight." Can my day get any freakin better? I have an overwhelming feeling this is going to be a very bad, bad idea……………

Three

Bani and I skipped school today to go shopping for some new clothes and to get our hair done. She repeatedly told me that I cannot, for any reason, put it up in a ponytail. "Fine, but if we get into a fight and some bitch grabs my hair and yanks it out, I'm blaming you, Bani."

She just puts on her most innocent smile, "Ok, you can do that, I won't mind at all if you blame me. I don't think we will get into a fight tonight though. We're there to have fun and maybe get lucky. Well at least I want to get lucky. You'll just be a tease." She smiled.

"I don't tease; I just don't sleep with every guy I run into." I said as we walk into another store.

"Ouch, that hurts, Cady. I don't sleep with every guy I meet. Sometimes I don't sleep at all." She said laughing.

"You're such a slut!" I said laughing with her. After what seemed like hours and a lot of changing into new outfits. We finally found what we were looking for, paid for it and headed back home. We got back to my house to get ready for my so called big day.

"We should get ready for the ritual before we get ready to go out, don't you think?" Bani said as we were walking through the front door.

"Oh crap, I was so busy shopping, I completely forgot about the damn ritual tonight!" Every witch has to have a mid-eve ritual with the moon just coming up on their eighteenth birthday. Everyone stands in a circle around five round flat stones, each facing north, east, south and west. The stone in the middle of the circle is represented as spirit. The stones stand about two feet tall and two feet around.

One stone for each of the five elements, earth, fire, water, air and spirit. In the middle of the forest chanting the old ways. You, the birthday girl go around and pass the wine for everyone to take a sip and say "blessed be my child" and then the b-day girl says it back to them. It takes forever to get to everyone.

"Man this is gonna blow, I can't stand these rituals, they're so boring. I don't know why we can't just skip out of it like we usually do. Hell, I can't remember the last one we went to," I whined.

Bani just look at me with what the-hell-look, "Oh shut the hell up and get over it. It's one freaking night and it's your birthday. You know this ritual is the only way you can get your full powers!"

"I…."she put her hand up as to stop me.

"Oh no, I'm not done yet. It doesn't happen very often that your birthday lands on Friday the thirteenth. To have a birthday on Friday the thirteenth is…. Is….You know that's like amazing in itself! So suck it up." She huffed.

"OK, ok I'm sorry! I know it's amazing and I'm proud to be a part of the witch world, you know that. You also know I don't like going to them, just like you don't like them either. Hell, it's usually your idea to sneak out of them and they're just so crowded with so many boring people," I argued.

She seemed to calm down and said, "I know it sucks, but we'll be out of there before you know it. We have to go to this one or you might not get your full powers."

All I could say was, "I know, I know."

"Then we can party all night long. Let's see how many guys we can get! Or should I say, I can get with!" Bani started running up the stairs, "Now, get your butt in gear, grab your robe and let's get this show on the damn road!"

We came down the stairs an hour later all dressed up in our nice maroon robes, ready to go to the ritual. Bani rushing around grabbing her jacket "Make sure you don't forget your goblet and amulet." Bani said with a smile.

"Yes mom, I have the goblet right here... See," I said with a tone as I held the goblet out in my hands "Umm and you know I never take off my amulet," I said.

"You know Cady, there's really no need to be an ass. I'm just making sure you have everything you need," Bani said with an equal amount of tone.

"Well Bani, this isn't the first ritual I've been too. I know what I need. In fact I've been to all the same ones you have. So back off and quit making me more nervous than I already am!" I was nervous, everybody was gonna be looking at me, hugging me and heaven knows what else they'll be doing. There were two people that I wish was there though, my mom and dad. Even though, I know that would never happen. They'll never be there or anywhere again.

"Cady, I'm sorry for being so bitchy. I guess I'm just as nervous as you are."

I gave her a hug, "Its ok. I know."

She hugged me back and then looked at me and with a sad smile she said, "Are you wishing your parents were here tonight?"

"Yeah I just miss them, you know? It's been five years since that day. Five years of knowing nothing about what happened to them," I said with tears in my eyes.

"I know you miss them and one day we will find out what happen to them. For just today though, this is your day and you need…. no, you deserve to have it all about you and only you, Ok?" She hugged me tighter, now with tears in her eyes too.

Again, that's why she's my best friend; she always knows what I'm thinking. Even if I don't want her to know. I thought with a smile, "I'm good Bani, really and thank you. Thanks for always being there when I need you." I smiled, "Now let's go get our ritual on, shall we?" We hooked our arms together and headed for the door.

We were taking Bani's 2000 BMW. She always says my 1969 Ford Mustang was too old. I had to keep reminding her it wasn't old, it's a classic. My dad was fixing it up to restore and to make everything on it look brand new. He was gonna give to me on my sixtieth birthday, but never got the chance. I read the 'repair and restore it yourself' books about cars and finished fixing it up myself. By the time I was sixteen, my car looked brand new.

We drove the twenty minutes outside of town. Hit the back roads that headed to the edge of the woods. We parked her car in a clearing by the trees. Neither one of us talked much on the ride here. I guess we both were just lost in our thoughts. I kept drifting back from the first day my dad told me what would happen once I got half of my powers.

He was a warlock and a powerful one at that, he could do anything with just a flick of his wrist. My mom was more shy when she did things though, you hardly saw her do any type of magic at all. I always asked what her main power was, but all she would say was that she would tell me when I older and could handle it.

"Firecracker, you're turning the big thirteen tomorrow, what wish are you going to ask for?" He always called me firecracker. He said it was because when I got mad I would hold it all in until I would blow up and let my mouth and fist explode.

"I don't know dad, I haven't really thought about it. I guess I'll know when I blow out the candles," I said laughing, "Oh wait! I know what I'll wish for…. My full powers and not just half of them!" I said still giggling.

"Firecracker, you better watch what you wish for? You just might get it." My dad said with a twinkle in his eye. "With my blood and you're moms blood running through your veins. Then there's the day and hour you were born. You'll have more power than you could ever dream of," he said, taking my hand in his.

"Dad, what will my powers be and how do I know if I even get them or how to use them? What are mom's powers? She won't ever tell me," I asked I wanted to know everything and I wanted him to tell right then.

"Firecracker, your mom will tell you all about her powers, but only when she thinks you're ready. For the other million questions you asked, it will all come naturally to you. You just have to be careful on how you use them in front of people. You don't ever want to use your powers in front of humans. They can never find out about what you are, that's why we picked Belton to live in. There are not many humans here. Now as for your powers, we'll start training the day after your birthday. As for today though it's all about you and having fun."

Right then my mother came in, "Cady, I would like for you to have this." It was the amulet she always wore. "This was passed down to me on my thirteenth birthday from my mother…and now I would like for you to have it." She put the amulet around my neck. It was a round, blue sapphire with a lightning bolt etched in gold in the middle of it. I have never seen my mother take it off.

"Now make sure you wear it at all times. It will always remind you of how much I love you and hope the best that life will bring you." She had tears in her eyes.

"Mom, I swear I'll never take it off and I'll protect it with my life."

It was the happiest day of my life. I was having a party, getting half of my powers and my dad was going to teach me everything I needed to know about magic. I couldn't wait to start training the next day. I never got to start my training though. They disappeared the morning after my birthday.

My dad's younger sister, Aunt Mable had come over that night saying my parents asked her to move in with me for a while. She would never tell me where my parents were or when they were coming back. She was about fifteen years older than I was. She had short black hair with a funny looking nose.

We lived in a five bedroom, three bath old Victorian style house. It had three levels with a bunch of hiding spaces. So it was always so easy to jump and scare Aunt Mable as she walked by. She would jump and scream, then notice it was me. She would continue down the hall muttering, "Horrible little witch." She didn't talk too much, if any, to me nor did she train me at all. So Bani and I worked on our powers together with Oma.

I figured out that I can make things turn to ice, and make things fly through the air with a flick of my wrist, like my father. That always made me happy to know that I got that from him.

We would use our magic to play tricks on Aunt Mable. Nothing we thought was really bad, but Aunt Mable never liked them. She was old and grumpy.

We would sneak out of the house and go hang out with a bunch of kids from school at the old mill at the end of town. I can't count how many times Aunt Mable would be waiting up when I came home way pass my curfew. She never said a word, just gave me a disappointed look and headed to bed.

Four

"Cady, will you snap out of your damn day dreaming. We're gonna be late!"

I blinked I didn't realize I was thinking so hard into my past, "Yeah sorry I'm coming," I muttered as I got out of the car. As we walked back through the woods, I could smell the pine cones in the fresh autumn cool air. The fire burning in the pots by the clearing was mixing with the breeze. Everything looked hazy through the light smoke. By the time we got to the circle everyone was standing around the stone in the middle talking. I walked up to greet the leader of the coven, Oma; she's also the owner of Elementz, where we work. She was standing by the stone, arms rising as she sees me.

"Catalina, there you are! I thought maybe you decided that you had better things to do tonight. Than hang around with all of us, old ladies?" She chuckled. Oma was one of the nicest, oldest witches I've ever known. She was like a grandmother to me. She is also the only one who ever calls me by my true birth name.

She has short black hair with grey streaks and for being a woman of eighty-nine years, she is very pretty and very down to earth about things. I always went to her for advice or just too talk about what I was feeling. She also was the one who helped me handle my powers. Since no one has ever seen powers like mine, Oma and Bani were the only people I trusted to tell what was going on. She wanted to take me in when my parents disappeared, but Aunt Mable wouldn't let that happen. I always wondered if I would have went with Oma how my life would've been different.

"No Oma, demons couldn't keep me away from tonight," I said with a slight smile.

She laughed, "Oh honey, no one could keep *you* from doing anything you wanted to do. Now young child, let's get the ritual started so you can go partying with your friends." She whispers with a snicker.

Oma and I stood in the center of the clearing with the coven circle and the five candles sitting on small stones around us. Each representing one of the five elements, earth, air, fire, water, and spirit. As we stood there, I looked around to all the other witches that surrounded me. To the left of Bani stood my Aunt Mable looking bored as usual, with her pointed nose and frizzy black hair. We made eye contact for a split second before she gave me a snide look. I never understood why she hated me so much. Sure, sometimes I put her through hell. It was all in fun though: besides, she was the one that was mean first. It really doesn't bother me that she hates me. All I care about is that I don't ever end up looking like her!

"Everyone gather around so we can get started please," Oma said. As soon as she starts talking everyone stopped to listen to her speak, she's just that powerful. "We are all here gathered tonight to celebrate Catalina Rose Ashferd's eighteenth birthday and the ascending of her complete powers. She was born on October thirteenth at thirteen-thirteen military time, on the day of the New Moon. She has shown great potential since the age of thirteen when the first half of her powers revealed themselves. It will be interesting to see what the fates have in store for this young, powerful witch." She glanced over at me, "Remember though with great power, comes great responsibility."

Oma took the amulet that was around my neck off and walked over to the first candle representing earth. As she lit the candle, she hung the amulet above the fire and said, "Earth be with you, Catalina." She walked to the second candle, air. She bent down, lit the candle placing the amulet above the flame saying, "Air be with you, Catalina."

She continued on to the third candle fire and lit it, hung the amulet above the fire saying. "Fire be with you, Catalina." As she continued to the fourth candle water, she placed the amulet above the flame.

I felt a light spark run through my body. Nothing to worry about though, I thought. "Water be with you, Catalina." Oma went to the last candle spirit. Bent down to light it, she placed the amulet above the flame, "Spirit be with you, Catalina."

Oma went over to pick up the goblet full of wine. As she handed it to me, she said, "May all five elements be with you, Catalina." She smiled and placed the amulet back around my neck. It felt warm hanging around my neck, but I was glad to finally have it back on. She handed me the goblet to pass around to everyone in the coven for the final phase of the ritual.

I first went to Bani, handed her the goblet as I said, "Blessed be, Bani."

Bani returning the smile took a sip of the wine and handed it back saying, "Blessed be, Catalina." I took the goblet and continued on to the next witch in line.

I smiled handed the goblet to Aunt Mable, "Blessed be, Mable." Aunt Mable took a sip, handed it back with no smile on that hideous face of hers.

With a harsh tone she said, "Blessed be, Catalina."

I continued on until I came to Oma, the last one I give the goblet to. I handed her the goblet smiling. "Blessed be, Oma."

Oma took the goblet to take a sip. She smiled handing it back to me, "Blessed be Catalina, may all your wishes come true." I took the goblet from Oma and took the last sip.

I held the goblet in both hands up towards the sky to saying "Blessed be, mother earth." As soon as the words left my mouth a lightning bolt shot down from the sky straight into my amulet.

I saw the sparks and felt the electricity run through my veins down my arms into my chest. That's when I blacked out. "Oh my heavens Cady wake up! Damn it wake up!" I heard Bani yelling and all I could think was, man she's loud.

I sat up looking around and saw everyone staring at me with worried faces. Well, all except Aunt Mable, she's nowhere to be seen. "I'm fine," was all I could say.

"Cady, are you freaking kidding! You're not fine! Lighting just hit you in the freaking chest!" Bani said with a worried panic tone, "Look at your arm!" she loudly whispered.

I looked down at my arm, my eyes went wide. What I saw made my head spin. I had a solid blue tattoo of a lightning bolt running down from my wrist to the middle of my forearm. It kind of looked cool; I looked over at Oma and asked, "Is this supposed to happen?"

"I don't know my child; I've never seen anything like this before. How do you feel?" She said with a sad look.

I thought about it for a minute. "I feel fine, actually I feel better than fine, I feel great. I haven't felt this good in a long time. I feel like I could run ten miles without breaking a sweat." I laugh.

Oma stood up and looked at everyone standing around, "Ok, the ritual is complete and Catalina is fine. We aren't sure about the lightning and the tattoo, but I'm sure it's what is destined for her. Everyone needs to return home and get a good night's rest. As I'm sure these two have plans of their own, that we don't need to interrupt."

I stood up, my legs felt a little shaky; I put one of my hands out on one of the stones to balance myself. I finally got balanced and started helping Bani and Oma gather up the candles.

"Catalina, sit down and rest, we'll get this," Oma said.

"Oma, I'm still not sure what exactly happened to me, but I'm ok. I felt little shaky at first, but I feel pretty good now."

She stood there with her finger to her lips thinking, "Well I'm not too sure what happened either. I'll look into it tomorrow and see if I can find anything out for you," she said with a smile. We finished gathering all the candles and put everything away.

Bani walked over to where I was, and she looked worried. She bent down and whispered in my ear so Oma couldn't hear her, "Cady, are you sure you're ok? We don't have to go out tonight," Bani said with a smile.

"No it's fine; really I want to go out tonight, Bani. Trust me it's all good," I said as I put my arm around her to head to the car. "Besides, it's not often that we get to hang out with Zane that much anymore," I said. We said our goodbyes to Oma and wished her well as we got in the car.

Bani piped up and almost shouted, "That is a freaking sweet tattoo! First your eyes are all glowing gold when you were pissed off and now you have a tattoo! I've never been the jealous type, but damn bitch, I'm jealous of you right now. You're gonna get all the hot guys tonight!" She laughed.

I just rolled my eyes. "You know, I'm glad you find me soo amusing. Sometimes you can be such an ass." Then we both started laughing.

Five

Bani and I pulled in my driveway, "Great, Aunt Mable's home." I said as we got out of Bani's car.

"Let's just get ready and wait for Zane in your room." Bani said as I went to open the door.

I opened the door, the first thing I saw were suitcases, "What the hell? You think she's kicking me out of my house?" I asked Bani.

Just then Aunt Mable walked down the stairs with another suitcase in her hand, "I see you're fine after you messed up the ritual. I'm not surprised through, I'm sure Oma stuck up for you and said it was some kind of destiny," Aunt Mable said snidely.

My eyes grew wide. I can't believe she's blaming me for what happened, "Aunt Mable, I had nothing to do with what happened tonight! I didn't make the lightning hit me! I could've of been killed and you just walked away!"

"Yes, well you're an adult now. You need to learn to deal with things yourself. Here" She said as she handed me an envelope. I held the envelope in my hand without looking at it. I was still shock on being blamed for getting hit with lightning. Aunt Mable continued talking as she picked up another suitcase, "You're eighteen and my job is done. I don't have to take care of you anymore and I don't have to stay here anymore. I'm finally done with you and your wicked ways. Goodbye," she said as she walked out the door.

I followed her out the door, "Are you freaking kidding me? You never took care of me! You never did anything for me! I did everything myself, I cooked, cleaned, I made sure I got up and went to school. You did nothing for me!" I kept yelling as she got into her car and drove away. As she turned the corner, I started to panic,

"How could she just leave like that?" I sat down on the front porch steps and started crying. Bani, sat down beside me.

I put my head in my hands, shaking it back and forth, "I never really liked Aunt Mable, she was never nice to me. But I don't think I did anything to deserve her just packing up and leaving."

Bani put her arm around my shoulder, "Cady, you didn't do anything to deserve this. This is all on her, she's just messed up. She always has been."

We sat there on the porch, neither of us saying anything at all; I was lost in my own thoughts. Someone pulled in the driveway, I looked up and for some reason I was hoping it was Aunt Mable coming back. It wasn't her, "Is that Zane?" I asked Bani.

"It looks like it. He must've got a new car." Bani said.

Zane was our other best friend; he's a half-demon. He's also our only gay friend. He can freeze things with his hands, like me. He about 5'8, skinny with glasses and cute in that nerdy type of way. He has short brown hair, with brown eyes. When he's in demon mode his eyes turn this deep purple, it's really cool to see. That's if you're not the one he's aiming at. He always fun to be around.

Zane got out of the car and walked over to us, he was wearing a pair of faded blue jeans and a nice button up shirt, "Happy birthday, Babygirl!" He said as he handed me a dozen pink roses.

I stood up giving him a hug, "Thank you, Zane." I said quietly.

Zane took me by the shoulders looking at me, "What's wrong, Cady?"

All I could do was just shake my head and cry harder. He wrapped his arms around me, squeezing me tight. Bani came over and stood by us, "Mable, packed up, handed her an envelope and moved out just now." She whispered to Zane.

Still hugging me he said, "Awe, Cady, it'll be ok. We'll get you through this. What was in the envelope?"

I hugged Zane tighter, "Thanks, and I don't know. I haven't even opened it." I wiped my eyes dry, pulled away from Zane and said, "I'm ok, I'm gonna go in and get ready to go out."

Zane and Bani both looked at me, Bani said, "Cady, we don't have to go out, we can stay in and rent a movie or something."

I shook my head, "No, I'm not gonna let her ruin our plans. If she wants to leave and never come back, well that's fine with me. It's not like she ever did anything for me anyway."

"Are you sure, Cady?" Zane asked.

I smiled, "Yeah, I'm sure. I'm kinda glad she's gone, at least now I don't have to walk around on pins and needles anymore." I turned and started walking into the house with Bani and Zane right behind me. I walked into the kitchen where the envelope laid. I picked it up and opened it, "Oh my heavens!" I yelled.

Both Bani and Zane came running in, "What, what's wrong?" Zane asked worriedly.

I handed him the check that was in the envelope, "It's over four million dollars!" I said breathlessly.

"Oh my heavens! What are you going to do with all that money?" Bani asked. "Well, we're gonna party tonight!" I said laughing. I put the check up in one of the canister on the cabinet. I will deal with that later.

I went upstairs to change out of my robe and into the new clothes I got today. I put on a pair of black jeans and a nice red silk shirt with a V-neck to show a little cleavage. I brushed my hair and was about to put it in a ponytail and then thought better of it. Bani would have a cow if she saw it up. I went to the mirror to put on my make-up. I applied my eye shadow to have that smoky look. Put on some light pink lip gloss and I was ready for the night.

I went back downstairs and into the kitchen, "Ready!" I said smiling.

We grabbed a sandwich and went out to Bani's BMW. Zane got in the driver side and we headed to the club to get our partying on! "Oh heaven help us, we're gonna get in trouble tonight!!" Bani said laughing turning up the radio as loud as it would go. We all started singing along to "Take it off" by **Kesha.**

Six

We pulled into the parking lot of the night club 'Jaggers' and it was packed with cars. "Wow, I wonder if they have a good band tonight?" Bani asked as we climbed out of the car.

"I'm just hoping we don't have to stand in line forever, it's kinda cold out here." Zane said as he wrapped his coat closer to his body.

"I just want to dance my butt off and get rid of all this tension. My nerves are still jumpy after the ritual." I said as I looked down at my new lightning bolt tattoo. Still wondering what in the hell it meant and what it has to do with my powers.

. "Evening ladies, how are you two doing on this lovely night?" the doorman asked. I looked up at him; he had to be at least 6'4. He was sitting on a stool, so I couldn't be too sure on how tall he is. Arms crossed over his broad shoulders, his black tight t-shirt matched his pitch black hair, which hung down past his shoulders. I looked in his dark brown eyes and for a split second I saw his true form flash before me. Whenever a witch comes into eye contact with another super natural, she can see his or her true form and this doorman here is a Demon. For that split second his eyes turned red, two horns sprouted out on both sides of his head and his teeth grew jagged, razor sharp.

"We're great! How are you?" Bani said with one of her sweetest smiles.

"I'll be better if I can meet up with you later. I'm Dirk," The doorman Dirk said, eyeing Bani up and down, landing his eyes at her chest.

"Well, buy me a drink later and we'll see what happens," She said as she put her hand on his knee.

"You're such a slut, Bani!" I laughed as we walk through the door. The strobe lights flashed all sorts of colors over a huge dance floor that covered half of the club. It was black and white checkered with a dance cage at each corner. I looked around stunned at how big this place really was. The bar itself was lined up against every wall. I guess that way you never had to wait in line for very long.

"Why don't you two go and grab some drinks? I'll find us a table somewhere," Zane said looking around.

"Ok will do!" Bani and I said unison.

We walk up to one of the bartenders waiting to order, "What can I get ya?" The bartender asked smiling. He had a nice smile with bleached blond hair, he must be out in the sun a lot. He had light blue eyes and golden tan skin. He reminded of one those surfer boys you see on TV.

I smiled just as nice at him as I looked into his eyes, he's warlock, nice. "I'll have a Coke. Bani, what do you want?" I asked looking over at her.

"Um, I'm not sure. What do you recommend, Mr. Bartender?" Bani said with her finger on her lips, like she's thinking. Oh lord that girl doesn't quit.

"I would recommend the jagger juice, it's my specially," The bartender said already getting my drink ready. Jagger juice is a combination of about five different energy drinks all in one.

"Sounds great! I'll take two of those and one coke," Bani said batting her eye.

"Ok comin up," He gave us our drinks and then handed me another coke. "Can you give this to Zane? Tell him it's on the house."

I took it smiling, "Sure will." Damn, Zane always gets the hot ones. We were trying to make it back to where our table was when I felt a hand grab my ass. I whipped around to see who was, but didn't see anyone who stood out like they did it. I shrugged, turned back around headed to our table.

"Hey Zane, the bartender said this was on the house." I said handing the drink to him while I slid into my seat with my drink.

"The bartender? Blond hair, blue eyes, nice looking guy?" He asked with a rise brow.

"Um yeah why, who is he, Zane?" I asked with a smirk.

"Oh his name is David. I hooked up with him a couple months ago. I didn't think he would remember me," He said with a shy smile.

"Honey, how could any guy forget about you? You're so damn cute!" Bani said as she pinched his cheeks on his face.

"Stop it Bani, you're gonna bruise me. Why don't you guys go dance and shake your butts off or something? I'll sit here and act like I don't know you," Zane said laughing.

"How about I just jump on you right here and give you one hell of a lap dance, in front of everybody. How would David like that?" I said as I got up. I stood in front of him, moved him and his chair so it facing me. I started dancing in front of him, inching closer to his chair.

"Cady, please don't embarrass me…..please," Zane begged.

I started laughing "Awe Zane, you know I love you," I said as I gave him a kiss on the cheek shaking my head laughing. I started heading towards the dance floor, "Come on Bani, let's go dance!"

We danced for hours with our drinks in our hand. Every time we went back to the table there was jagger juice waiting for us. You gotta love it when the bartender likes your best friend. Our drinks were never empty. I flopped down in my chair, put my head down on the table and whined, "Oh my heavens, I'm soo tired of dancing!"

Zane just started snickering. "Well you guys have been dancing for like ever. Why don't you just sit down for a while?" Zane asked. "Here David brought over another drink for you."

I lifted my head off the table just enough to look up at him, "Zane, I'm glad David likes you and all, but damn can't he just ask you out? He brings over drinks every five minutes just to talk to you… Don't get me wrong, I'm glad we don't have to pay for all these jagger juices we've been drinking. Oh and happy that he likes you and all, but damn." I said putting my head back down on the table, "I don't think I can drink another one, it might just come back up." I was starting to feel a little light headed and dizzy.

Bani, was walking up to the table, with four guys. This is not what I needed right now. "Hey where did you go Cady, I thought you were still dancing?" As if I answered her she went on. "These guys are having a party at their house. They want to know if we wanted to come with them and make it a real party?" she said holding one of the guys hand.

"If you're having a party, why are you here at the club then?" I asked eyeing each of them. Zane kicked me under the table and Bani gave me the 'shut the hell up' look. I looked at both of them, "What? I just wonderin."

One of the guys sat down next to me. He put his hand on my knee, giving it a little squeeze. "We just came here to see if we could get any hot girls, like you two. Do you want to come back to our party? You would make it a lot more fun."

I grabbed his hand from my knee squeezing hard enough to make his eyes water in pain, "Unless you want to lose your hand, I suggest you keep it to yourself." I let go of his hand and he stood up backing away. Hiding behind one of his friends. "I don't think I want to go to any party Bani, but you go and have fun," I said smiling.

She bent down giving me a hug, "Ok, well then I'll call you tomorrow." She turned to leave with all four guys trailing behind her.

"You think it's ok to just let her go with them? We don't know who they are or where they even live. What if she gets herself in trouble?" Zane said in a worried voice.

I shrugged, "Nah, she'll be fine. She can take care of them if she has to. It wouldn't be too hard for her, they're all four human."

I see Zane sit straight up with a huge smile on face. I looked over to see what he was looking at. David the bartender was walking towards our table.

I smiled, "I'll be right back, I have to go to the bathroom."

Zane frowned, "Ok, but don't take too long. I don't want him to think I just sit here all by myself...all the time."

As I got up I passed David, he had a really sweet smile while he was looking at Zane.

I pushed my way through the crowd of people to get to the hall where the bathroom was. The bathroom was at the end of a dark hall, around the corner. Then you have to walk into another room just to get to the bathroom.

I finally made to the bathroom, looked at myself in the mirror, "Oh crap Cady, you look horrible!" I said. I was still a little light headed, but I just chalked up with too many energy drinks. I was sweating from dancing all night. My hair was tangled into a mess and my eye make-up had smudged under my eyes. I grabbed a paper towel to wipe under my eyes to get rid of the smudges that didn't belong. I took my fingers and kept running them through my hair to smooth it out, "There, that's better," I said smiling.

I opened the door to walk out, looking down smoothing my shirt down. I ran right smack into a huge, hard chest, "Sorry" we both said at the same time.

I raise my eyes to meet his. He had dirty blond hair that hung to his shoulders. His shirt was tight around his broad chest, pointing out how muscular he was. He had the brightest emerald green eyes that I ever seen. They met mine. We stood there just staring at one another, neither breaking contact. There was something about him, but I couldn't put my finger on it. As I looked into his eyes, I saw his true form was a wolf. That brought me back to my senses.

My mom always told me to stay away from wolves. She said witches and wolves don't mix well. After she disappeared, Aunt Mable continued to tell me to stay away from them also. I was never allowed to be near them. So I've stayed away from them as much as possible.

I looked away mumbling, "Excuse me."

He kept his eyes on me, "No problem." I snuck a peek back at him. He had the most prefect smile, straight white teeth with dimples on both sides of his cheeks. His ash blond hair came to his shoulders. My knees became shaky, the pit in my stomach was on fire.

He gave me one more look and turned, heading to the men's restroom. As he walked away, my eyes traveled down. My heavens, even his butt is perfect! Too bad he's a wolf, I thought shaking my head.

I was almost at the end of the room before I got to the hall, when someone popped up in front of me, "What the hell!" I screamed and jumped back. Then I got a look at who it was. "Eddie, what are you doing here?" I said in angrily. Eddie, the ex-psycho half-demon boyfriend, who that tried to burn my car up with me in it. He has brown hair with brown eyes, nice looking, but a jerk from hell.

"Hi Cady, how are you?" he said with his smug smile.

"I'm fine, now move out of my way," I really can't stand him. We only dated for a couple of months and he had our whole lives planned out, I was just having fun. I wasn't looking for a future, especially with him. When I told him that, he went psycho and tried to kill me.

"Oh, come on now Cady, is that anyway to greet me?" he said coming closer to me.

"Yes. Yes it is, you tried to kill me Eddie! How else am I supposed to *greet* you?" I said through gritted teeth. Before I could blink he was inches from me. I stepped back and hit the wall.

Man, he was quicker than I remembered. So I did the only thing I could think of. I brought my fist back to swing to hit him. He grabbed my wrist, so I tried with the other fist. He now had both of my wrists in his one hand, pinned over my head to the wall. I tried to force them down, but he was to strong. "Let me go now, Eddie!" I shouted.

He brought his hand up, sliding his finger down my cheek. Wrapping his hand around my neck, "Damn girl, you're still as sexy as I remember. By the way happy birthday honey…I've missed you." He brought his head in closer, forcing his lips on mine. I tried to move my head to the side, his grip tighten around my neck.

I thought I was going to throw up. I had to get away from him. He was trying to force his tongue in my mouth. Finally, I let him. And, I waited. Then I bit down hard on his tongue. He jerked his head back, spitting blood.

"You little bitch, you bit me!" He slammed my head into the wall, I saw stars. "You're gonna pay for that Cady, I was trying to be nice." Like he was ever nice. "But if you want to play rough, then that's what it will be!" He slammed my head into the wall again.

I tried to get my hands free from his grip, I tried using some magic. Nothing seemed to work. Something was wrong with my powers. Well when magic don't work, try physical. I tried kneeing him. He moved just in time. He just laughed, "Honey, what's wrong? Why don't you use your powers on me?"

He somehow flipped me around where my face was smashed up against the wall and my hands were now behind my back. He pressed himself up against me, rubbing his hand up and down my side. He started rubbing between my legs.

"It's ok honey; I know why you can't use your powers on me. In fact I know why you can't use your powers at all. I slipped a little something in your drink to help block you from using them," he whispered in my ear as his rubbing became harder. I had to get out of this now.

"Yeah Eddie, that was pretty smart of you. You always did think of everything." I'm thought I was gonna puke my guts up just thinking about being nice to him. But it worked as he loosened his grip on my hands.

I took a deep breath in and threw my head back, hitting him in the face. He gasped, and lost his grip on me.

I whipped around to where I was facing him. I head butted him again right in the nose. Blood started gushing, but I wasn't done. I spun around and kicked him in his gut. He was now on his knees holding his gut. I thought about hitting him again, just to make a point, but I decided to just get away from him for now. I still don't have my powers yet, thanks to him.

I went to run out of the room and three guys blocked my way. Or should I say two demons and vampire. "Get her, and bring her ass back here!" I heard Eddie yell from across the room.

"You boys really don't want to do that." Someone growled. I turned to see who was talking. The hot wolf that went into the bathroom was now leaning up against the wall with his arms folded across his chest. Ok this is good, he might be able to help me with these assholes. That would make if four against two, not good odds but doable. Eddie now stood and looked at the wolf. "You better just mind your own business. This has nothing to do with you, dude," Eddie said through gritted teeth.

"Name's Chase, and if she wants me in her business, then that's where I'll be." He said with a smug smile.

Chase looked over at me, as if to say, it's up to you? "Well hell yeah, I want you in my business." I said as I looked over at Eddie, smiled and gave him the middle finger. Well, that pissed him off.

Seven

Eddies eyes became fire red, flames dripped from his fingertips. This is gonna be fun. All of sudden I went flying. Hitting the wall with so much force, I thought my head was going to snap off. I sat up shaking my head trying to focus and quit seeing double. I looked around.

"Who's the jerk that just hit me?" I shouted. One of the demons popped up in front of me.

"That would be me, sweetheart." He said flashing his yellow eyes. I hate yellow eyed demons, they're just messed up.

"Ok, just wonderin whose ass I had to kick." I said as I kicked him, he went flying. The second he got up I was ready. I hoped my powers were working. I threw three ice balls at him at once, oh yeah they're back. Weak, but at least I they're back somewhat. Two of the ice balls missed, but the third hit his shoulder.

I looked over to see Chase and Eddie still fighting. It looks like Chase was winning. I was hit again and went flying through the air hitting the wall, again. My vision went blurry, I was trying hard to focus.

Zane burst through the door, "Cady, what the hell!?" Zane said running into the room, his eyes glowing deep purple, he was pissed.

Right before he reached me, Zane didn't see the vampire appear behind him. The vampire grabbed his throat, opened his mouth and sunk his teeth into Zane's neck. "ZANE!!!"

Zane's eyes went wide with shock. He couldn't seem to move. The vampire had him by the neck with one hand and had the other was around his chest crushing him. Zane was already starting to turn pale from the blood loss.

Zane grabbed the vampire's arm that had a hold of his chest. He focused all his energy on freezing the vampires arm.

The vampire still had a hold of Zane's neck and chest, his fangs in his neck sucking his blood. It didn't matter what Zane was doing, the vampire wouldn't let up.

I pushed my way up from the floor. My head throbbing, trying to focus on getting to Zane, before that freaking vampire drains him. I made it to my feet and started towards him. Again I was thrown into the wall. I don't know how much more my head can take getting hit like that.

I didn't let it stop me though, I had to get to Zane. Eddie appeared in front of me grabbing my throat, throwing me across the room. I hit the floor hard, my head hit the wall. I felt the blood run down my head into my eyes. My vision was getting blurry again.

I tried to focus my vision, I saw Chase. He was fighting both demons now, and having a hard time with them. I can't think about him right now. I have to get to Zane and Eddie is the one standing in my way.

I stood up, feeling unsteady on my feet. I held my arm up, palm out, ice balls shot out towards Eddie. He disappeared, I looked around. Where the hell did he go?

I felt something hard smack in the back of my head, I dropped to my knees. I started to black out. Eddie yanked my arms behind my back with a tight grip. He grabbed a handful of my hair, pulling my head up.

"I want you to watch him kill your best friend, Cady." He said sneering, "He's going to drain him dry, and there's nothing you can do about it, but watch." He cackled an evil laugh. That brought my senses back, I struggled to get out of his grip.

He was right. There was no way I can get out of his tight grip. It was hard enough to try and keep my eyes open. I tried to push frost out of my hands, but he had them to where it was freezing my back instead of him.

I locked my eyes with Zane. His blazing purple eyes were starting to fade back to brown. He kept his hold on the vampire arm, as it froze. Zane yanked his hand down with all his might. The vampires arm snapped off and fell to the floor.

That didn't stop the vampire though, he just bit into Zane's neck harder with a grunt. Zane was losing, "Please Eddie, don't do this! I'll do anything, please just make him stop, please!" I cried. I felt my eyes tingle, I looked down and gold tears were rolling down my face.

"You should've thought about that before you bit me." he whispered in my ear, "Don't worry honey, I have plans for you too. Just much worse than what's happening to your little gay friend over there." He chuckled. "But it will still be fun...for me that is."

Zane's eyes were now changed back to brown, his head fell forward hanging down like he's praying. I knew then he was dying, or already dead. The vampire then threw Zane's body over his shoulder like a bag of potatoes, looked over at me and smiled. Blood dripping from his fangs...Zane's blood, then he ran out the back door. "I'm going to kill you." I said to Eddie in a calm voice.

I felt the rage build in me, energy started flowing throughout my body. I felt the sparks run through my veins down to my fingers. My eyes started to tingle and I knew they were changing into pure gold. I flew my head back causing Eddie to lose his grip on me. I stood up, looked down at my hands; electricity was dripping from my fingers. Eddie now standing, we locked gazes and for a brief moment he looked stunned. "What the hell is wrong with your eyes!" he asked with a shaky voice. I didn't hear what he was saying.

"I told you Eddie, I'm going to kill you," My voice calm. I raise my arm palm out, never taking my eyes off him. Feeling the electricity running down my arm as lightning bolts shot out of my palm into his chest. His eyes grew wide in a state of shock before falling to the floor. Eddie laid there convulsing a few times, smoke coming off his body. He better be dead is all I can think of as I walked towards him. I stood over his body and kicked his shoulder; he was lifeless and still smoldering. Good.

I was heading to the back door to go after Zane. He might still be alive. I almost made it to the door, when I was hit with something in the head again. I fell to the floor, I looked up to see one of the two demons that were left, he kicked me in the gut and I went flying. The other one ran over from where ever he was and they both picked Eddie's body up and ran out the door. "No!!" I stumbled as I tried to get up, but my body hurt. I didn't care, I had to get Zane from that vampire. I tried to stand once again, but fell down.

Chase came running over to where I was lying. He looked as beat up as I felt. His lip was bleeding, cuts all over his face down his arm. His shirt was shredded into pieces, "Are you ok?" he asked breathing hard. I tried to push myself up, he grabbed my arm to help me.

I shook him off and started stumbling towards the door they went out of.

I pushed open the door and staggered outside. Looking around, there was no one there. I fell to my knees crying uncontrollable "Zane!! NO….NO….NO!!!" He was gone, "Those sons of bitches took him, NO…Zane!!" I put my head in my hands and cried I couldn't stop. He's gone and there was nothing I could do. It was my fault, I couldn't save him. He was there because of me, because he was worried about me. Because of that he was dead. How could this of happened? Not to Zane, he's never hurt anyone.

"I'm sorry about your friend, but we got to get out of here. They'll be back any minute." Chase said.

I felt numb and I didn't want to move, I didn't care if they came back and killed me. Chase reached down and gently picked me up, "Sorry, but we got to go." He said quietly. I didn't say anything, I just cried. All I wanted was Zane. I knew that he wouldn't be there anymore and the more I thought about it the more I cried and hated myself for letting him die. I should've saved him somehow, someway. Some powerful witch I turned out to be. It didn't do me any good when I needed it most.

Chase carried me over to his car. Laid me down in his back seat. I could feel the vibration from the car. We drove for hours it seemed.

When we stopped he got out, opened the back door reached in pulling me out. He carried me up some steps and through a door. He walked up some more stairs and gently laid me down on a feather top bed. I felt a cold rag go around my neck and my head. I laid there still crying, and when I couldn't cry anymore, I finally fell asleep.

I was dreaming of Zane, *watching him die over and over again. Watching the life drain from his eyes, Eddie laughing the whole time.*

"This is your entire fault Cady. You know it didn't have to be like this. You could've saved him, but you're too weak! You'll never be all powerful like they said you would!" I looked away and saw Zane, he was holding his neck.

"Cady, why didn't you help me? You could've of saved me, but didn't. You just sat back and watched. You let this happen to me. You're the one who killed me, it's was your fault and I'll never forgive you!" He yelled, his eyes started blazing purple.

"No Zane! I tried to save you, I swear I tried! I'm so so sorry. I love you Zane, I swear I tried!" I cried.

Zane laughed alongside of Eddie. They both started throwing fire balls at me. I was able to dodge them all. I looked up and all of a sudden Zane was in front of me. "This is what you did to me, Cady." He smiled and I saw for the first time, he had fangs. They turned him into a freaking vampire!! He open his mouth and tore at my throat.

"NOOOO!!!!" I was screaming.

Eight

"Cady, wake up!" I woke up with Chase shaking me, with worried eyes.

I grabbed my throat to make sure it was all intact. "I....can't....breath...I," I gasped.

"You need to calm down and take long deep breaths." Chase said has he looked into my eyes. I took a long breath in and started coughing, my throat hurt so bad. "Here drink some water, but just take sips." He handed me the glass.

I got my breathing under control enough to take a sip; my throat felt like it was on fire. I handed him the glass and fell back against the pillow. "How long was I sleeping?" I asked in a raspy voice after I got my breathing under control.

"About fourteen hours, give or take. I was going to let you sleep longer but you started screaming in your sleep. So I thought I should wake you up." He shrugged. "You can rest some more, and I'll go make you some food. I'll bring it back up here when it's ready." He got up and headed to the door.

"Chase" He stopped and turned to look at me. "I just want to say… thank you. Thank you for everything." I said uneasily.

He grinned when he said, "No problem at all, I'm… I'm just glad you're ok." And he walked out the door, shutting it behind him.

I lay there looking around the room. It was simple, white walls, a dresser by the wall and a closet. Another door that I assume is the restroom. I looked over to my left and there was a door that went out to a balcony. I got up out of bed, went to the door and stepped out on to the balcony.

I was amazed by how beautiful it was. The leaves had started falling from the trees. What was left on the trees were the most vibrant colors of brown and orange that I ever seen. The river ran down past the trees, and from what I could see, was crystal clear, I could hear a waterfall in the distance. It was like no one had ever been here to mess it up.

I was thinking about everything that happened last night. When the hell did I get the power of the lightning bolt? I wonder if it has anything to do with my tattoo on my arm.

"It's beautiful out here isn't it?" I jumped, whipping around nearly falling over the rail.

Chase caught my arm and pulled me close to him. "Whoa, be careful, I don't want you falling over," He said with a grin. "Sorry, I didn't mean to scare you. I brought you some food and a change of clothes," He said still holding my arm, our bodies touching. I could feel a shock as our bodies touched.

I looked down at myself, I noticing I blood stains all over my clothes. "Thanks, I look and feel like crap." I said with a slight smile.

He just chuckle, "You should eat."

We went over where a small table with two chairs sat. He made fried chicken, mashed potatoes, gravy and corn. Wow, not only is this wolf hot, but he can cook too. Damn I hate the rules that say witches and wolf can't hook up!

Right then my stomach growled and I realized how hungry I was. We sat down at the table, I still couldn't get mind off of Zane. This couldn't be happening.

"What are you going to do now?" Chase asked.

I guess he wants to get rid of me already. That's ok, I should leaving anyway, "I guess go home and get a hold of Bani and tell her about Zane," it hurts just to say his name. I took a deep breath and continued, "And then go over and talk to his parents…. After that I'm going after the blood sucking ass that *killed* my best friend." I was getting pissed with every word that came out.

Chase was shaking his head. "Cady, you killed Eddie. He was a very powerful demon, but his dad is ten times more powerful, and he has a lot of demons behind him. You can't just go up against that!" Chase demanded.

Who's this guy think he is? "Don't tell me what I can and can't do! I know how powerful Eddie was and I know who the hell his father is! Eddie's dad will understand after I tell him what his son did! If he doesn't like it, I'll kill him too. I can take care of myself!" I shouted.

Chase pushed his chair back, stood up. Came over to where I was seated, bent down and got right in my face. He spoke slowly and in a low growl, "Do you honestly think for a freaking second, that his dad cares what his son did? He won't think twice about killing your ass!" He stood straight up and starting walking back into the house yelling the whole way. "You're not going anywhere, end of discussion!"

I pushed my seat out fast and hard, the chair flew and hit the wall. I yelled as I followed him inside. "Who the hell do you think you are?"

He whipped around and pinned me up against to wall, slamming his hands on the wall next to my head. He came inches to my face, his glowing green eyes glaring into mine. In a low angry growl he said, "I'll tell you who the hell I am. I'm the idiot who saved your dumbass."

I could feel his hot breath with every word. He was breathing heavily. I should have been scared, but surprisingly I wasn't. I glared back at him, "What? I'm just supposed to hide and run away? I don't do that! I'd rather die fighting, than running away like a coward! And I didn't ask you to save my 'dumbass'" I felt my eyes feel with tears. I was frustrated, mad, and let's face it, scared. But I pushed them down. I refuse to cry in front of this jerk. I could feel my eyes tingle, they must be gold by now.

Chase closed his eyes, took a deep breath. He never moved away from me. His breathing relaxed, opened his eyes. He looked at me for a moment with concern, "Cady, I understand that you want to go after the vamp that killed your friend. Really I do, I would want to do the same thing if some bastard hurt someone I cared about. You have to think about this. Eddie's dad will come after you with all his demons and when he gets a hold of you…. you will wish he would just kill you. He'll make you suffer. It will be worse than any death…."

He thought for a minute before he continued, "I know it's in your blood to want to fight. Please…I'm asking you, let me help you? At least let us come up with a plan or something together?" He pleaded.

Why does he care what happens to me? He doesn't even know me. I'm sure Eddie's dad will probably make me suffer. I met the guy once and he didn't like me the second he laid eyes on me and I did kill his only son. I'll be screwed if he gets a hold of me, but I still just can't let it go.

I took a deep breath, "Ok, we'll come up with a plan, but I have to go back to at least make sure everyone's ok." I was starting to calm down, "You didn't happen to grab my phone did you?" I asked hoping he says yes.

"Sorry, I didn't see your phone," he said still not moving.

"Oh ok...that's ok." Crap I was starting to panic, "After I get everything, where am I supposed to go? Everyone I know or even care about is in Belton. So what am I supposed to do, just leave town and never come back? And what about school? I have school Monday. Am I just supposed to drop school? I'm supposed to graduate in December." I am really starting to get scared now.

He must've been thinking about it, but he finally smiled, "Ok... You can call your family, I have a phone. I'll take you back to get your stuff, but it's going to be in and out that's it. Gotta it?" He slightly smiled, "We'll also check on your friends, then we'll come back here and figure out what to do next." Chase looks at me with sly eyes, "Oh and just to let you know, we're not in Belton, anymore."

I must've looked shocked cause his smile grew, "We're in the mountain of the Ozarks. So no one will think to look for you here. There aren't any neighbors for miles. You'll be safe...I will protect you, I promise. As for school though, we'll have to figure something out." He looked so heartfelt, but I don't trust very many people. Particularly guys, especially were-wolf guys.

"Ok, so we're not in Belton, got it. By the way I can take care of myself. I've been doing it since I was thirteen, and I have no family. I have my best friend and that's it." I looked up into his eyes, "But, why…Why do you want to help me? You don't even know me." I asked uncomfortably.

He stepped back, brought his hands down to his sides. Looked away before answering, "I don't know I… I just feel it's the right thing to do that's all." Then he walked out the door.

Ok well that was weird, wolves are so touchy. I guess I will get started on the plan then.

Nine

I walked around the room for a while. It was starting to get kinda late, so I decided to take a shower. I grabbed the clothes Chase gave me, a pair of sweats and sweat shirt. "Well this is sexy." I muttered to myself as I walked into the restroom.

I turned on the hot water, stepped in the tub and let the water wash the blood and pain away. I was washing my hair when I found the large lump on the back of my head. I looked down at myself, I was covered in bruises and cuts. I looked like I got the hell beat out of me last night, well I guess I did.

My mind went to Zane, but I pushed it away. I didn't want to think about him right now. Then my mind went to Bani. I bet she's worried sick about me right now. I never went over twenty-four hours without talking to her. I wonder if she knows about last night yet. What if Eddie's dad goes after her to find me? What about the coven? He could slaughter them all because of me.

If I thought Eddie was a worthless piece of shit, his dad was ten times worse. He hated me the second he met me. He said something about me being an abomination, or something like that. I thought he was just a jerk. I don't know what I'm going to do, but I have to keep Bani, Oma and the rest of my coven safe.

There was a knock on the door. "Cady, are you ok in there?" Chase asked through the door as he knocked again.

I shut off the water and stepped out if the shower wrapping up in a towel, "Yeah, sorry I guess lost track of time. I kinda used all your hot water," I chuckled uneasily.

"It's ok I already took a shower. I was just making sure you were ok." I went to answer him, but I heard the bedroom door shut.

I really don't understand him, I thought to myself. I got dressed, looked in the mirror. I noticed I had a cut on my forehead that someone had taken care of with butterfly stitches.

I went back out into the bedroom and sat down on the bed. I started brushing my hair, "Ouch! Son of…" I said through gritted teeth. I jerked my brush back and put my hand up to the back of my head. I forgot about that huge lump on the back of my head. It hurt like hell, no wonder my head was killing me.

Chase throw open the door and ran in the room, looking around. "What's wrong?" he asked questionably.

I jumped up looking around, what did I miss. "Nothing's wrong. Why did you come barging in like that for?"

He looked at me confused, "I heard you scream."

It was my turn to look at him confused. "I didn't scream, I quietly said ouch. I hit a bump on my head, which I forgot about." He seemed to calm down looking at me.

"A bump? I don't remember you having a bump on your head when I laid you down on the bed last night. Let me see it," He headed towards me.

I put my hand out in a stopping motion. "It's fine, my brush just hit it, that's all. Really it doesn't even hurt.... that bad." Even though it did and my head still hurt like hell. He must have sensed it, because he didn't stop.

He walked up to me and gently placed his hand on the back of my head. I clenched my teeth. "Sorry, it's a nasty bump, does your head hurt?" I nodded yes. He left his hand on my head and looked into my eyes. "Maybe we should have someone look at it? I don't know much about head wounds, but you might have a concussion."

I smiled, "I'm a big girl with a hard head, I'm sure it will be fine. Besides you said I couldn't see or talk to anyone. So who would you suggest look at my head?"

Chase devilish smile right back at me, "Besides a psychiatrist?"

I grinned, "No dumbass, you told me I shouldn't see anybody. So how do you suggest I get the bump looked at? Do you have some medicine man hiding in your house or something?"

Apparently what I said was funny, because he started laughing. He wasn't even going to try and hide it. He does have a sexy deep laugh though. He tries to hold back his laugh and says, "No, I don't have a medicine man hiding anywhere. I was thinking more of my pack leader, he's kinda like a doctor."

Oh, ok now, I was feeling like the dumbass. "Will it be ok that he knows that I'm here? I don't want to cause any more trouble for you or your pack." I said genuinely concerned.

"Well honestly, I was hoping that I didn't have to get them involved at all. However, I really think you should be looked at, you could get worse."

I looked up to meet his eyes, "I really don't want to cause any trouble and it's just a bump on the head. I have a hard head, it'll be fine." We stayed that way, neither one moving or breaking eye contact.

Then like a flash Chase looked away and headed to the door. "I'll go call him and have him come out tomorrow to have a look at you." He said in a hurry. Why does he always do that? He must really not like me being here at all. I know I said it before but, werewolves are so touchy. That must be one of the reasons my mother always said to stay away from them.

I walked around the room for a while longer, it was a plain room and I was getting bored and it was getting dark. I decided to go out to see where Chase was. Maybe he finally came up with a freaking plan. I opened the door and walked out into the hall. I stood there looking around. I was on top of some stairs, it looks like there's only one room up here.

I started walking down the stairs. I could see the living room, it had a couch, chair and TV. There's a fireplace in the corner, but nothing else. No pictures on the wall, no end tables, nothing. There is a door to my right probably leading outside and a door on my left, I assume is the other bedroom, maybe his parents. There was a little doorway leading into the kitchen. Well, I hoped Chase was in there.

As I walked into the kitchen I could smell the aroma of something cooking on the stove. The smell was making me hungry. Chase was stirring something on the stove.

He turned his head smiling slightly. "Hey, I see you finally made it out of the bedroom. I was going to bring up some food for you. Since you're down here, pull up a seat to eat." He pointed to one of the chairs at a nice little kitchen table.

I sat down, being nervous about everything. I'm not sure why I was so nervous, so I pushed it down. "So is there anything I can help you with?" I asked.

He grinned carrying over two bowls, handed me one and took the other one and sat down. It was a chili, my favorite.

"Nope already done, but thanks anyway." We sat there in silence eating our chili. When all of a sudden Chase spoke up, "I called my pack leader. He'll be here some time tomorrow morning. How's your head doing since your shower?"

I thought for a minute before saying, "Fine, it hurts a little still, but other than that it's good. Oh, by the way, thanks for fixing the cut on my forehead. You did a really good job on it, and for the clothes."

Chase looked up and smiled, "It wasn't a problem at all. My dad taught me how to fix people up a long time ago. As for the clothes, sorry they were the smallest I could find. They kinda hang off of you...a lot."

"Oh they're fine. I'm just glad I could get out of my blood stained shirt." I said nervously. As I sat there I wondered if his dad is the pack leader, "So is your dad the pack leader? If you don't mind me asking?" He sat there for a moment not saying anything or even looking up at me.

"No, I don't mind and no, he's not the pack leader, my dad is dead. He was killed about two years ago, when I was seventeen," He said as he got up from his chair taking his bowl to the sink to wash it out. He turned his head towards me.

"Well it's starting to get late. We'll head back to your house after Garrett, that's the pack leader, says you're ok." He looked uncomfortable, "Um, there's just one problem though."

I looked up at him confused. "Only one problem?" I smiled, "What more could be wrong?"

He chuckled, "There's only one bed here… I could take the couch… I guess."

It was my turn to laugh, "No, take your bed, I've seen your couch. You couldn't sleep on it and be comfortable. I'll take the couch."

He thought about for a minute before he spoke again, "We can just share the bed. It's a king size, if you're ok with it, it'll be fine with me." Chase said.

It was my turn to be uncomfortable, "Umm, sure, it's fine with me, I can sleep anywhere," I said.

"I'm gonna go get ready for bed then." He started walking out the kitchen muttering more to himself "This is gonna be a long night."

I got up from the chair and went to put the bowl in the sink shaking my head the whole way. "Men" I chuckled.

Ten

I headed up the stairs, went to open the door to the bedroom, but then thought twice about it, as I didn't want to walk in on Chase naked, well maybe I did a little. I knocked on the door and waited.

"Come on in." Chase said through the door. I open the door and walked in. Well he wasn't completely naked, but almost. He had a pair of boxer shorts on and nothing else. Yup this is gonna be a long night.

He looked over at me with a sly smile, "I can give you a shirt and pair of shorts if you want?"

I thought about it for a second and put a devilish smile on my face, "Oh thanks, but I sleep naked….is that ok with you?"

I didn't know wolves faces could get that red. "Um....well....I...I guess if what you want to wear is nothing its fine by me."

I started laughing, "I'm kidding, and the shirt and shorts will be great. Thank you."

Then he got a sinful smile on his face, "Ok, but don't be surprised, if I try to rip them off of you in the middle of the night then. Cause....I'm ok with you not wearing anything at all. In fact I would prefer it." He said looking me up and down.

It was my turn to get all red in the face. He just snickered, went to his dresser and pulled out the clothes for me.

I went to the bathroom and put them on. The shirt was way too big and hung down pass my knees. The shorts just kept falling off so I decided they're staying off. The shirt was big enough where they hung down to my knees and you couldn't see anything. I walked out the bathroom. Chase gave a slow wolf whistle.

"Don't be getting your hopes up or anything. The shorts you gave me kept falling off, so I figured this will have to do." I raised my brow, "And try and stay on your own side of the bed," I said with the cockiest attitude I could come up with.

"I make no promises. I can't even say I'll try." Chase said with an even cockier smile. Man, this is gonna be a long freaking night, I whined in my head.

I went to lie down on one side of the bed as far over as I could get. Chase jumped in the bed next to me, slid over to where we were barley touching. He brought his arm around my waist; I could feel the electricity as we touched. I inched over a little until I was hanging at the very edge. I turned my head slightly in his direction.

"Back off, wolf boy," I said with a sly smile.

He took his arm away and put back to his side, "Awe don't be like that, I just want to cuddle," he whined.

"Yeah, well I have a headache. So no cuddling for you tonight or any other night," I said as I put my hand over my head and turned over to my side.

"Oh, I'll get you to cuddle with me," he said cleverly.

"Hey, I heard you muttering to yourself, about 'it's gonna be a long night'. What was all that about?" I said holding up my fingers in quoting marks.

He chuckled, "Yup, that's what I said; not saying it was gonna be a long night for me." He shrugged, "I was just saying it was gonna be a long night for you."

I raise my brow at him, "Why would it be a long night for me?"

Chase smiled, "Are you gonna let me tear your clothes off of you?"

"Umm no," I said.

He shrugged, "See, it's gonna be a long for you then. Cause I don't think I can keep my hands off you the whole night."

I smiled a sweet smile, "If you like your hands, then I'd suggest you keep them to yourself." He just laughed quietly.

I was laying there for a while still thinking about everything that has happened today, "Hey, can I ask you something?" I asked quietly.

"Sure what is it? If you're gonna ask if I will take my shorts off....the answer is yes." Chase said in a low sexy voice.

I laughed quietly, "No it has nothing to do with your clothes. I was going to ask you about what you said earlier, that it was in my blood to fight. What made you say that?"

He laid there in silence for a moment before he spoke, "I don't know, I guess it just seems like you're a type of person that fights for what she wants."

"Then why did you say it? I mean someone just doesn't say, 'I know it's in your blood to fight'," I said in a deep voice, "So again really, why did you say it?" I asked. He laid in silence for what seemed like for hours.

Until he finally spoke up, "I guess... I don't know if when I tell you...Will you please not get all girly and pissed off at me?" Well this doesn't sound too good.

I turned to look at him, "Ok, I don't get girly and I won't get pissed off."

He turned to his side with his head propped up on his hand looking at me, "Umm, well you smell different." I just stared at him in shock. Did he just say I smelled?

"Before you start yelling, let me explain," He took a deep breath, "Wolves can smell different senses on people, witches, demons, humans and other wolves. Everybody has a scent to them. Yours though, I've never smelled before. I know it sounds weird and all. I thought I knew every scent. Yours, well I've never come across before, that's all."

I laid there thinking about what Chase just said, "Oh, ok, I think I understand. I smell different. Well that's little odd, but anyway, what do I smell like? Cause you would think I would smell like a witch."

His gaze met mine, "You have the scent of the witch, but there's also another scent to you too. I can't tell you what it is cause like I said, I've never came across of that scent before....sorry if I'm not making any sense," He said with a guarded smile.

"Ok I get it, I was just wondering. At least you can smell the fight in my blood." I laughed trying to lighten the mood, "Night Chase." I said as I turned over to where I wasn't facing him and closed my eyes.

"Goodnight Cady, sweet dreams." Chase said in a whisper. I lay awake for some time just thinking. As I lay there I could feel his breath on the back of my neck, breathing deep and even. He must already be asleep. I finally fell into a deep dreamless sleep.

Eleven

I woke up to find myself half on Chase. I was lying on my side with my head nestled in his neck. One of my legs was intertwined with his, and my arm was around his waist. Chase had one arm under my neck, and his other hand rested on my hip.

As quietly I could I started getting up. Chase wrapped his arms around my waist and pulled me back, "I told you I would get you to cuddle with me," he chuckled.

I hit him in the shoulder, and started getting up again, "I did not cuddle with you, now….get off me."

Chase chuckled again and pulled me down next to him, "Hey, you're on me, besides, I'm not ready to get up let's just stay like this for a little while longer."

I shook my head, "Yeah well, I want to win the lottery. Neither will happen, now get up." If I was being honest with myself. I could just lie here all day and not think about anything. Lying next to Chase was pretty good too. It felt safe, right and natural.

"Fine, if you're not gonna stay and cuddle with me, can I at least take a shower with you?" Chase asked while he climbed out of bed. I stood there looking at him with nothing but his boxer shorts on. His chest looked as if he worked out all day and night. He also had a tattoo of a wolf's face on his upper chest. His biceps were hard and toned. Looking up at his face, his emerald green eyes looked, bright and beautiful, staring right back at me. He reminded me of my dream man.

He smiled a wide grin showing his dimples and straight white teeth. He raised his brow, "So does that mean yes about the showering together?"

"In your wet dreams, wolf boy," I said as I turned and headed to the bathroom, "And don't think about coming in here while I'm in the shower."

"You know you want me!" He yelled as I shut the door. As I let the water wash away everything that's been building up inside me over the past couple of days, my mind kept seeing Zane's face and that horrible dream.

"Hey, are you going to use all the hot water? Or did you decide to let me in, to take one with you. You know to save on water and everything?" Chase said though the door.

I turned off the water put a towel around me and headed out the door, "All yours, have fun." I said smiling.

"Babe, you better put some clothes on….your killing me here," He said in low voice as I passed him. I just smiled and kept walking.

"Looks like a cold shower will do me some good," He growled as he walked into the bathroom to take a shower.

I looked around to find my clothes. I found my jeans which were in ok shape. My shirt on the other hand still had blood all over it. I went over to Chases' dresser to find a shirt, they all looked huge.

I finally found the smallest one I could find and it was still big. I put it on, tucked it in my pants the best I could. Just then Chase walked out of the bathroom wearing another pair of boxers. Man he looks good standing there with his hair wet and messy. He went over and got a pair of jeans out and put them on.

He turned and looked me up and down, "My shirt looks a hell of lot better on you, than it ever did on me."

I looked down at his shirt that I was wearing, "Huh sorry, I couldn't get the blood out of mine," I said shyly.

He chuckled, "No I was being serious its looks great on you." He walked over to where I was, we were now standing toe to toe. I could smell the soap and aftershave coming off of him. We stood there gazing into each other's eyes. He put his hand behind my neck coming closer to me. I couldn't look away and I didn't want to.

We were inches from each other now, in the back of my mind I heard my mother say. *'Cady I want you to always stay away from wolves, they're no good and you'll end up getting very hurt. They're sneaking and very dishonest; they'll do anything to get what they want. They're nothing but evil'.*

I turned my head and backed up, "Um, I think I heard the door," I said as I opened the bedroom door and headed down the stairs. Man, I can't let him get to me. I thought as I sat down on the couch. . I looked up when I heard Chase coming down the stairs, I looked away quickly.

He came over to where I was sitting. He was leaning up against the wall with his arms crossed over his chest with his head down, "I'm sorry Cady, and I didn't mean to scare you or upset you in anyway."

I turn to face him, he looked worried, "I'm fine. I just thought I heard the door, that's all." I said nervously.

I put my head into my hands, my head was pounding. Chase came over to where I was sitting. He bent down with concern in his eyes as he asked, "Are you ok? Is your head still hurting?"

I nodded, "Yeah, not as bad as yesterday, but I can still feel it throbbing," I said honestly.

He came close to my face and whispered, "Let me have a look at your head." Chase brought his hand up and gently placed it on the back of my head never taking his eyes away from mine. "You have remarkable eyes," Chase said quietly.

He brought his other hand up to the side of my cheek. I wasn't sure what to do. I know I wanted to feel his lips on mine. I also know that I shouldn't trust him or even be with him at all.

My mother drilled that into my head from birth, Aunt Mable after her. Luckily there was a knock on the door. We both looked over to the door. Chase sighed and got up and walked over to the door. I let out a breath that I didn't realize I was holding.

Chase opened the door and an older man walked in. He looks to be in his mid-sixties with grey hair. He's built like a linebacker. Chase talked to him quietly when they both looked over at me. Chase waved me over, "Cady, I want you to meet Garret, the pack leader."

I walked over and held my hand out, "Nice to meet you, Garret." He took my hand in his bringing it up to his mouth. I thought he was going to kiss my hand, but instead he smelled it. Whoa, this is weird. I don't think that has ever happened to me before. Garret inhaled deeply and then let my hand drop.

He stepped back looked and snarled his nose and spoke for the first time, "Chase, you are not to help this *Valkyrie*," he roared, "She's a *Rota; she'll* cause nothing but turmoil to whoever she meets." I glanced over at Chase, he had the same look of shock that I felt.

Chase spoke up first, "Garret, what are saying? I'm going to help her, she needs it. There's people after her."

Garret's faced reddened, "Good, let them have her. You will not help this...this girl. She can deal with it herself and that's an order!" he yelled. Ok, this guy is just pissing me off.

"Who the hell do you think you are? I don't cause turmoil or any other kind of trouble, and I'm not a Valkyrie, or whatever it is you called me! I'm a witch, one that can kick your freaking ass!" I felt my eyes tingle, so I know they turned pure gold. I looked down at my hands and I could see electricity dripping off my fingers, I stepped towards him.

I felt hands on my shoulders. "Cady, you need to calm down and take a breath," Chase whispered in my ear.

"Look at her eyes! Pure evil!" Garrett howled.

"Garrett, shut the hell up and let me handle this!" Chase growled.

I shrugged out from his grip, whipped around and facing Chase, "No screw that! I won't calm down and I can handle myself! In fact, you know what? It's fine. You stay here and take your orders. I'm going home to find my friends."

Chase grabbed my hand, "Cady, please just calm down. Let me talk to Garrett." He pleaded. I glared hard at him for a moment. I looked into his pleading green eyes.

My breathing calmed down and I could feel my eyes going back to normal. I took a deep breath in and relaxed. I gazed into his eyes and said calmly, "No, I'm sorry Chase, he's right I need to deal with it myself. That's what I should've done at the very beginning. I told you, I didn't want to cause you any trouble and I already have." I had tears in my eyes.

I turned to walk out the door. I looked over at Garret; he had a smirk on his face that I would love to knock off. I opened the door, "Sorry, Chase," I said as I closed the door behind me. I heard Chase say something, but I couldn't listen I just had to get away from there.

Twelve

I ran down the driveway thinking town can't be too far off. A few miles or ten, I run two miles a day this won't be too hard. I kept running down the drive until I finally got to the end of it. There was a path to my right, woods to my left. Well if I'm smart about it, I'll stay on the path. As I thought about this though, I didn't want that jerk to pass me on his way out and gloat. I decided to take the woods. It'll be like a short cut.

I started running through the woods. Ducking under branches, climbing over shrubs and logs or tress that has fallen, at least it's downhill. It was getting cold, I should've grabbed my jacket.

I ran for what seemed to be hours. When I finally stopped, I looked up at the sun above me. It has to be about noon now, that jerk showed up about nine this morning. So

I figured I'd been running and walking for about three hours now, and it was getting colder.

The town can't be that far off, there's no way I missed it. I know little if anything about the Ozarks. It has mountains everywhere and that's about all I know. The town itself sat in the middle of it. It's not a large town by any means. Still it can't be that far, I just keep telling myself.

I was walking, looking at the ground so I wouldn't trip over something, when I heard something behind me. I slowed down so I could pay attention to the noise. It sounded like limbs breaking, a gust of wind blew hard around my face. I looked up and there was a man standing there.

As I looked at him in the eyes. I noticed he was a demon, with yellow eyes. Great, just what I freaking need now.

Most yellow eyed demons have the power of telekinesis, they can move shit with their minds. I can't stand that kind, their usually bad tempered and just plain mean.

"Hello there little girl, are you lost? Or just looking for some fun?" He asked in a shrewd tone.

I held my ground, "Nope, I'm not lost and believe me when I say, I'm not looking for any type of fun. Especially with you," I said with sarcastic tone.

"Aww, now, you hear that Curt, she doesn't want to have any fun with us?" He said looking behind me.

I turned my head to see who he was talking to and, yup, there was another one behind me.

He smiled a cricked smile, "Well that's too bad, cause we want to have fun with you." Just as the last words came out of his mouth, he jumped towards me. I immediately threw my arm up, palm out. I could feel the frost forming on my fingers. I shot out an ice ball, which he dodged quickly.

"Whoa, she's not just a little girl, she's a witch. Ohh, this will be fun then," the first one said. I stood in my fighting stance where I could face them both. Arms up, palms out waiting to shoot some more at them.

"I don't want to fight you, but I will if you make me and I will win. Just to let you both know. Now if you leave, we can all continue on our separate ways," I said hoping like hell they decide to leave. No such luck though, the second one, I believe was Curt threw fireballs at me. I dove away from them, barely missed me.

I heard a crack above. I looked up just in time to see part of the tree fall right at me. I threw my palm up, I could feel the electricity flow from my hand. Lightning hit the tree bursting it into flames. As I was looking up both demons came flying towards me, one of them hit me in the shoulder. The other one luckily missed me.

I kicked that one. Curt went flying into a tree. I glanced over to where he flew, he was out cold. Good. Now I can focus on the other one. He snarled, "You little witch, you're going to pay for that!"

All of a sudden limbs, rocks and I can't see what else, came flying at me. I dodged most of them, but a few hit me. One nailed me in the head and I went down on one knee.

My head will never be the same after all these blows I've been getting lately. One thing about demons, they're a cocky bunch. "Oh come on now, is that really all you can do? Throw things at me? Really, that's just lame. I would be embarrassed, if I was you," I said as I got up.

"You haven't seen nothin yet. I'm gonna have so much fun, messing you up," he said with a sly smile. He threw another log at me, I dodged it easily.

I jumped up and ran toward him, did a summersault over him. Then kicked the back of his knees, he went down. I then punched him in the back of his head. He fell to the ground face first, hopefully dead. I heard a grunt behind me, I whipped around and smiled to myself.

Chase was behind Curt twisting his neck, breaking it. "Thought you might need a little help here, babe," he said with a cocky grin.

"Nope, I think I had it all under control," I said with a smug grin.

"Yeah, well, while you were focusing on that guy," He said pointing at the demon lying on the ground in front of me. "This guy was about to throw a fireball at your ass." Chase said pointing at Curt.

"Oh…well, then, thanks for the help again. I'll be leaving now." I started walking in the direction I was heading before I was attacked.

"Cady, can you hold on for a sec? We need to talk," He said as he ran to catch up with me.

I didn't stop, I just kept walking. I really didn't want to talk to him. He caught up to me grabbing me by the arm, turning me to face him. "I said I needed to talk to you," he growled.

"Don't you dare growl at me, go back home Chase. I can handle this myself," I said through gritted teeth.

"Then don't walk away from me!" Chase demanded. He gripped me tighter, pushing me back up against a tree.

"Let me go!" I said trying to get my hands free.

"Not till you stop and let me talk, please," He pleaded.

"What, what do you want to talk about, Chase? You can't help me, I know that. I'm ok with it, really I…I am," I said in an unsteady voice.

"I want to help you, Cady, I know what I want and that is to help and protect you," he said in a confident voice.

"You don't need to protect me and you can't help me. Your pack leader, made that very clear," I said.

He stood there with his hands still on holding on to my arms. He stepped closer, his body pressing up against mine. His lips were so close to mine that they brushed against them. He whispered, "I don't care what he said. I told you that I would help you…. I want to help you."

Damn his bright green eyes, he looks so good. I can't figure out why my mother never wanted me to be near any werewolves. Maybe they're not all like she said. Garret maybe, but not Chase.

"I don't want you to get into any trouble," I whispered.

He laugh quietly, "Let me worry about that, ok?"

I nodded, "Ok."

His lips brushed against mine. "Does that mean you'll go back with me then? Or can I keep you like this for little while longer,"

I said stepping out of his grip, "OK, lead the way."

He followed behind me laughing,

Thirteen

We started walking back towards Chases' house. "How did you find me?" I asked.

"I'm a werewolf, I tracked your scent," he said like I should've known.

"So how did you talk your pack leader, *Garrett,* into helping me?" I asked slowly.

He kept looking straight ahead, "He's not helping you...I am." Well what does that mean?

"Oh ok, sooo how did you get him to let *you* help me then?" I asked quietly.

"How the hell did you walk for three hours and not get very far?" He asked changing the subject.

"Hey I thought I was going the same way as that damn path," I argued.

He chuckled, "Why didn't you just stay on the path? I mean it's about fifty miles to town, but at least you would've made it there before dark."

I stopped in my tracks, "What? What do mean fifty miles? I thought it might be around ten or so. But fifty miles? Are freaking kidding me?"

He turns to look at me smiling, showing his prefect teeth and great dimples, "I told you, we were in the mountains of the Ozarks."

I felt like an idiot, "I thought when you said, mountain of the Ozarks…It wasn't literally in the freaking mountains."

He chuckled; "I figured you knew."

I was steaming, "How the hell was I supposed to know where the hell I was? I do believe I was passed out, when you brought me here." I said impatiently.

"Well, maybe you should have asked then. Are you always this bitchy when you don't know something?" he asked prickly.

"I'm not being bitchy! I asked a freaking question, that you thought was hilarious. So excuse me for not liking to be made fun of!" I was fuming now, "You're such an ass." I said as I started walking away.

He stepped up closer to me, "I'm the ass? I've been trying to help you every way I can. You have no idea what I have gone through or what I'm gonna have to go through to help you! And you're calling me an ass?" He growled.

He stepped even closer to me to where I could smell his soap and aftershave. I backed up and he kept getting closer, I was backed up against a tree.

He fixed his eyes on me as he came closer. Our bodies were now touching. "Ok I'm sorry. I know you've been helping me and I appreciate it very much, really I do. I also know that I'm being bitchy, and I'm sorry for that. I just want to get home and make sure everyone's ok," I said defeated.

He brought his lips down inches from mine, "I'm sorry too, I didn't mean to sound like an ass. I'm just frustrated right now, but thanks for saying that." His lips now barely touching mine.

I could kiss him or walk away. Listening to my mother, I decided to walk away. I turned my head, "We should really get going."

Chase gently took a hold of my head and turned it back towards him, "Cady, why won't you let me kiss you?" He asked with compassionate eyes. I knew why I couldn't kiss him. I didn't want to get hurt and I knew that's exactly what would happen if I let myself kiss him.

"Why do you want to kiss me so bad?" I asked nervously.

He smiled saying in a very thoughtful tone, "I've wanted to kiss you from the moment I saw you."

"Well, you can't kiss me. I...I heard about you and...and your kind." I said timidly.

Chase looked at me puzzled, "What exactly did you hear about 'my kind'?" He asked.

"The only thing wolves will do is get me hurt. They also say that they're ruthless and will lie to get what they want. That...that I needed to stay as far as I can away from them. And that they would kill me rather than look at me. My mother was the main one to say all this. She also said how evil they are." I said looking down at the ground. I couldn't look at him. He had been nothing but nice to me.

"Cady, look at me," Chase took my chin in his hand and made me face him. "I want you to look me in the eyes and tell me you think that about me."

I looked in his beautiful green eyes, no I couldn't say that about him. He's been nothing but polite to me. He even saved my life. Here I am pretty much calling him a ruthless bastard. Nice Cady.

"No, I don't think that about you. I….I just don't know what to think anymore. My mother drilled in my head about how evil werewolves were since….I don't know, since birth," I said still looking into his eyes.

"Cady, please trust me……no not trust." He said shaking his head, "I know you have some trust issues that are going on in that pretty little head of yours. All I'm asking is that you please try and see a different side of me, than what your mother told you. I want you to see me….the real me." he kept his hand holding my chin staring into my eyes, "I won't ask you to trust me…that I will earn from you. You will see I really do want to protect and help you." he said with heartfelt eyes.

He kept starting into my eyes, "I know that I really don't know you and you don't know me. I just feel pulled to you, as if I want….no, need to be with you. If that makes any sense at all," He said shaking his head, "I'm not making very good sense at all am I?"

I wanted to trust him, I just didn't know if I could, "Ok, no, you're really not making any sense at all," I said chucking. As I looked at him, I understood exactly what he was saying, because I felt it too. I just didn't want to, or have time, to admit it to myself. Not right now anyway.

I smiled, "I'll try to trust you, but that's all I can do right now. Please try and understand where I'm coming from with all this?" I asked tentatively.

"That's all I'm askin for, babe," he said smiling. "So does this mean yes on the kiss?" he asked raising his brow.

I put both hands on his chest, smiled and then pushed him back away from me. "Not today, wolf boy," I said laughing as I walked away.

"Ouch, you're killing me, babe!" Chase said has he caught up with me, "Can I at least hold your hand?" he asked in a shy tone.

I glanced over at him and saw him smile with his cute dimples. "Ok, but your hands better not be all clammy and crap," I said rolling my eyes and still giggling.

He grabbed a hold of my hand, intertwining his fingers with mine. "You're such a romantic, Cady," he said sarcastically bringing my hand to his lips, kissing each finger.

"So why did Garrett call me a Valkyrie?" I asked, acting like I didn't notice the tingles going throughout my body. Just by holding his hand, and by him kissing my fingers.

He kept walking, shrugging, "I don't really know, to be honest with you. It might be your scent. I told you it was different." He glanced at me, "He has a lot of old books and has met a lot of different people. Maybe, he came across a Valkyrie before and thought you had the same scent." He said shrugging.

"Why the hell would I have the same scent as a Valkyrie? Hell I don't even know what a *Valkyrie,* is. I'm a witch not…not that, man he's a dumbass." I said frustrated.

Chase just laughed squeezing my hand, "It'll be fine, and we'll figure out what it all means together." He kissed my hand again, "For now, just consider your blood special."

We walked a while longer in silence, when we came up to Chase's driveway. "Shit, I thought we had more time," Chase said muttered. "Cady, listen me very carefully, ok?" he asked.

I looked at him, then at the seven guys standing in his driveway, "OK… what's going on Chase?" I asked confused.

He looked at me with pleading eyes, "Please, just listen to me. Go get in the jeep, lock the door and whatever happens just…..just drive away. Go to town, don't look back, I'll meet you there. Ok?"

"What the hell is going on?" I said worried. I looked at these guys and saw the pack leader, Garrett. Well, shit, what's he doing here? I thought he would've left by now.

We started walking up the drive. The guys looked at us and not a one of them smiled. We got to the jeep, Chase squeezed my hand and said through gritted teeth, "Get in, lock the door and go."

He opened the driver side door and I got in. He walked over to where those guys where, they seem to be talking. Well, Garrett was talking mostly. They were all standing in a circle around Chase.

All of sudden one the guys swung his fist back and hit Chase in the face! His head flew back, but he stayed on his feet, then another one hit him. This guy knocked him to his knees. Then most of them started hitting and kicking him, all but two of them. Those two were just standing there with their heads down.

Chase wasn't fighting back at all. I sat there watching in horror! I looked over at Garrett, he was standing there with a smug look on his face. I couldn't take it anymore. I opened my door, got out and I started running towards Chase.

"Stop!" I yelled. I was just about to Chase, when one of the guys grabbed me. I swung around and punch him in the face, he flew back a few feet. I turned to keep going, trying to reach Chase. Another one of those jerks kicked me to the ground. I got back up, and I could feel my eyes changing to gold, I was pissed. I held up my arm, palm out aiming right at Garrett.

"Cady" Chase said in a whisper. I looked over at him and we locked eyes, "Don't…just let it happen." He said through clenched teeth.

"You want me to stand here and let them beat the shit out of you? Are you freaking insane?" I shouted.

"Yes…please don't do anything," he whispered, closing his eyes.

I stood in horror, watching them kick the shit out of Chase. While two guys had a hold of me by the arms. I couldn't watch anymore so I looked away, tears running down my face.

"He has to do this…it's our way," One of the guys whispered in my ear. I didn't say anything back, all I could hear were the hits making contact and the grunts Chase made. He never said a word, just took everything they gave.

It seemed to go on forever, when I finally heard Garrett speak up. "That's enough…let's go." That was all he said. He walked past me, stopped and looked at me. I wanted to punch that smug look off his face, but the two guys still had a grip on me.

"How could you do this...he's in ...he's in your pack? Why...why, would you do this?" I couldn't get all the words out, I didn't even want to look at him.

"He made his choice...and he's no longer in the pack. He picked a Valkyrie over his pack. He's all yours now." He roared as he walked away.

"I'm not a Valkyrie you senile old man!" I yelled, as he got into his car.

The two guys that had a hold of me let go. As they walked pass me, they still had their heads down. One of them slightly looked over at me, "Sorry, we didn't want to do this." He whispered. They all loaded up in their cars and left.

I ran over to Chase, who was lying on the ground. I dropped to my knees, "Are you ok?" was all I could ask.

He looked up at me and smiled, "I've been better....I thought I told you to stay in the jeep?"

I still had tears running down my face, I quickly whipped them off. "Damn it Chase, why did you let this happen? Why did you let them beat the shit out of you?"

"Only way," was all he whispered. Then he passed out, I tried to get him to stand up. He was like moving a boulder! Great! I put both of my arms under his arms and started dragging him inside.

I got him up to the door and he finally woke up. I helped him to his feet, and through the door. We made it to the stairs, and I practically had to drag him up. I finally got him to his room, I laid him on his bed. I turned to go get a wash rag to start cleaning off the blood.

He grabbed my hand, "Cady."

I turned and looked at him, "I'm not talking to you," I said as I went to get the rags.

When I got back his eyes were closed, his face was swollen already. He had a cut over his eye and on his lip.

He had cuts and bruises on his chest and arms. He looked horrible.

He opened his eyes and looked at me, his bright green eyes looked pleading, "Cady, don't be mad at me." I really didn't know what to say.

"I'm not mad at you," I said with a slight smile. "But what the hell were you thinking, Chase? What happened?" I asked.

"I told you, it was the only way." He said.

That was not the answer I wanted, "Don't lie to me Chase, and don't sit there thinking I'm some dumbass that doesn't know crap! So I'm going to ask you one more time, what the hell just happened?" I said through gritted teeth.

He laid there in silence, then finally spoke up, "Fine, this morning when you ran out, Garrett told me to make a choice. So I did, and he didn't like the choice I made." Chase said shrugging, never taking his eyes away from mine.

"What choice?" I asked.

He took a deep breath, "The choice was either I was with the pack or with you…. I chose you." he said and then quietly more to himself, "I'll always choose you."

I was speechless, I had no clue to what to say or do. So I did the only thing I could think of, I smacked him upside the head. "Ouch! You know they did hit my head. What was that for? I said I choose you." he said as he rubbed his head.

I sat down in front of him, "What the hell were you thinking? I'm not the dumbass. You are," I stated. "You left your pack for…for me." I said in barely a whisper.

He took my hand in his and gazed in my eyes and said in low sly tone, "So can I get that kiss, now?"

I started laughing and smacked in the arm, "You're such an ass…" was all I got out. He grabbed me and pulled me close to him. He brushed his lips next to mine, never taking his eyes away from mine.

"I'm only going to kiss you, if you say I can. I'll never do anything, you don't want me to do." I didn't answer him, I just brought my lips to his and started kissing him.

There was a second of shock on his face, but he quickly recovered. His kiss was slow and passionate, his tongue came out tracing my lips. I opened my mouth, letting it in. Our tongues met in the middle, intertwining with each other. It was like this was what they were made for.

I could feel the electricity flowing between us. I couldn't tell if it was my powers or if we were making it, but I liked it….a lot. My whole body tingled with delight, I felt heat in the lower part of my body. I pulled my head slightly back keeping his lips on mine. "Just making sure it was worth it?" I asked breathlessly.

He growled a low growl and pulled me even closer to him, "Oh, I knew it was worth it and so much more." He said, just as breathless. He went to kiss me again, neither of us could get enough of one another.

I finally pulled away and went to stand up. He pulled me back down on him.

"Stop it. I have to get you cleaned up, you're kinda gross lookin." I said wrinkling my nose at him.

He chuckled, "I heal fast, you know?"

I started walking to the bathroom to warm up the rags. I looked over my shoulder, "Yeah, you might heal fast, but that doesn't get rid of all the blood that's on you." I walked into the bathroom and shut the door, turning on the water. My heart was pounding so hard, I thought it might jump right out of my chest.

What am I thinking? How did I go from supposed to stay away from werewolves to not getting enough of one! I shouldn't be making out with one of them and really liking it might, I add. My mother would kill me if she was here. She was very clear on staying away from them. As for why to stay away, I'm not sure. Maybe things and people have changed since then. Maybe she was hurt by one. I don't know, but I think I just might wait and see where this thing with Chase goes. I'll just not get in over my head and fall for him completely, if at all. That's what I will keep telling myself anyway.

Fourteen

"Hey, you know I could be bleeding to death! You ok in there?" Chase yelled from the other room.

I got the rags from the sink, turned off the water and walked back out. "Umm yeah, I waiting for the water to warm up, it was taking forever," I said quickly.

He was standing up with his torn shirt off looking all too good. I quickly looked away, "Here's a washrag for your face." handing him the rag.

He grabbed my hand and pulled me close to him, wrapping his arms around my waist and putting his forehead on mine. "I'm sorry about what happened out there. I didn't want you to see that. I really thought we'd be gone before he got back," Chase said miserably.

I wrapped my arms around his neck, "Chase, why did you choose me over your pack? You don't even really know me." I asked quietly.

He smiled, "If I tell you, will you promise me something?"

I raised my brow, "Umm, promise you what?"

"Promise you won't run away screaming, or hit me again?" he asked warily.

I stood there thinking, "Ok, I promise I won't run away screaming. The hitting you, well that I can't promise. You might need it."

He chuckled, "Ok, I guess I can handle that." He took a deep breath in and held it, like he was trying to get the courage to say something. He let go of me and walked over to the balcony. He looked outside for a long time then finally turning to look at me. He rubbed his face and pushed his hair back, putting his hands on the back of his head.

I stood there staring at him, "Are you going to tell me or just walk around all day?" I asked with my brows wrinkled.

"I don't know how to tell you, without sounding like some psycho," he said quietly. "Ok here it goes, you're my mate. I saw you at the club and I just knew we belonged together." He was talking so fast, "I can't explain it much because it has never happen to me, but I do know that we belong together. A true wolf has one mate and one mate for life and I always considered myself a true wolf. I don't do one night stands, in fact I haven't slept with anyone. Hell, I don't even go to the clubs. My pack brothers drug me to that one I met you at. I'm glad they did now, but at the time I bitched about it the whole way there."

He rubbed his hands through his hair again. "Lying with you last night, I….I knew then with all my heart and soul that I wanted to be with you and only you." he took a breath.

I stood there wide eyed just staring at him, "Chase I…"

He held up his hand, "No, please just let me get it all out Cady. Ok…. I feel what you're feeling. I don't know how or why I can but, I do. I felt it just now when you kissed me. I felt the electricity running through my body….. Garrett told me to stay the hell away from you and your kind. He wasn't talking about witches, he kept saying you're a Valkyrie. When I told him that you said and believed you were a witch, he said the hell you were. He said you were a Valkyrie and well…Cady he said he knew your mom and she's a Valkyrie also."

"That's when he told me to choose between you or the pack. I didn't hesitate when I chose you. That's when I ran out to go find you. Cady, I'll never hesitate when it comes to you…… Now with all that said, I know I was talking really fast and probably didn't make much sense if any at all. I just wanted to……no, I needed to tell you. I will understand if you want to leave, I won't stop you or stalk you." he said has he looked at me.

I sat there wide eyed staring at him. "Umm, Cady, are you going to say anything at all?"

I was still wide eyed staring at him. What was I going to say? I can't think straight. "Wait, what did you say?" I asked.

He looked at me with a puzzled look, "Umm, which part?"

I threw my hands up in the air, "The part where you said Garrett, knew my mother?"

Chase looked at me confused, "Really after all that I just said, that's all you're going to question?"

"No, of course not, I'll get to the rest," I said biting my lower lip. He stood there watching me, I guess waiting for me to say something.

"I don't know what to say, Chase."

He had a hurt look in his eyes, "You don't have to say anything." He grabbed some clothes and headed towards the bathroom, "I'm gonna go take a shower." With a hurt expression in his eyes he passed me and went into the bathroom shutting the door behind him.

Well, I just screwed that up. I sat down on the bed and thought about everything he just told me. My mother was the first part that popped in my head, I pushed it away. I'll think about that later. Right now I needed to figure out what Chase said about me being his mate.

I felt the electricity between us and now I know he felt it too. How I do feel about being his mate? What does that even mean? He did pick me over his pack, he got the hell beat out of him over me. What the hell was he thinking?

We're going to talk about this and we're going to talk right now, damn it! I got up from the bed, marched over to the bathroom door, threw it open and yanked back the shower curtain. "We need to talk about all this right now!" I said.

Chase's eyes grew wide, "Umm, Cady, can we talk about this when I'm done?"

I looked at him, then I looked down and realized he's naked. I couldn't think, "We….umm… we to…" I kept looking down then back up at Chase. He was grinning from ear to ear dimples in full cuteness! "Aww hell… will you at least cover up?" I shouted.

He looked around, "Sure, can you hand me a towel?" I grabbed a towel, throwing it at him and stomped back into the bedroom. I was so embarrassed! How in the world could I forget that detail of him being in the shower? Not to mention the fact he was going to be naked. I sat down on the bed and put my head in my hands shaking it back and forth.

Chase came out of the bathroom coming over to where I was sitting, "So, what did you want to talk about?" Chase asked still sounding dejected, looking down at me.

I peeked through my fingers, yup he's just in a towel. "Aww man, you still don't have any clothes on." I whined

"Well, I was kinda in the middle of taking a shower....what do you want to talk about, Cady?" I had it all in my head what I wanted to say to him. Now I have no idea what to say.

"I..." I took a deep breath, this is going to be hard to say, "I'm sorry... I'm sorry for leaving you hanging like that after everything you said. It wasn't like I wasn't listening or anything like that. It's just when you brought up my mother and said Garrett told you he knew her and she was a Valkyrie, I kinda got sidetracked, and for that I'm sorry. It's just that I've been looking for her for five years."

He sat down beside me, "I'm sorry, I didn't know."

We sat there in silence for a while, I finally spoke up, "So what is this mating thing? There's not some kind of ritual is there?"

Chase chuckled, quietly and said, "No, there's no ritual you would have to do. It's just pretty much what I've told you from the beginning, I'll always be here for you to help and protect you. Well, to…just be with you, I guess." He still wouldn't look at me.

 So I kept asking questions, "What if it doesn't work out with us?"

He glanced over at me, "I know it will work, for me at least, but if you ever want out, you just walk away, I guess."

I thought about it for a minute, "Would you hate me if I did?"

He turned and faced me at that, "Cady, I would never, couldn't ever hate you. No matter what happens between us, if anything was to happen," Chase said sincerely.

"I don't know about the mating thing, I....I've never had... I've never had sex." There I said it, "I've never had sex so I don't know how to 'mate'." I said putting quotation marks on mate.

Chase looked taken back, "I thought you and that Eddie guy had...umm... You know I just thought you had. I mean it's great if you didn't, I just thought you had. But anyway that's not what being a mate is all about, it's about just being together."

I laughed, "Umm, no, he tried and we did other things, but never had sex." I shrugged, "I didn't want to have sex with someone I knew I wouldn't stay with. That's one of the reasons we broke up. He didn't like that answer."

I know I really liked Chase, but I'm not sure what it all means. As if he was reading my mind, he took a hold of my hand and said, "Cady, I don't want you doing anything you don't want to do. I didn't tell you any of that to get anywhere with you. I told you, cause it's how I feel and I wanted you to know, that's all."

"Thank you Chase, can I think about it for a while?" I asked softly.

He rubbed his thumb over my hand gently, "Cady, you can take all the time you need or want. I'll be here, I'll always be here for you."

I turned to look at him, his big green eyes shining. I bent over and lightly kissed him on the lips, "Thank you Chase. Now go finish taking your shower. You still have blood on you and it's still kinda gross."

He laughed, "Ok, soo are we good then?"

I snickered, "Yeah, we're good."

"So can I still kiss you?" he asked in a sly tone.

I raise my brow looked him up and down and said, "Oh, well, hell yeah, you can kiss me all you want."

I didn't have to say anything else, Chase took a hold of my chin and pulled me to him. Our lips met in the middle and it felt like the most natural thing to happen. Chase's tongue gently slid over my teeth and into my mouth, our tongues intertwining with each other. I felt the electricity flow through my body.

He broke away from the kiss, but kept his lips inches from mine. He whispered, "I should really go take that shower now."

"Yeah, you really should," I said brushing my lips to his.

Chase pulled his head back and stood up. Shaking his head smiling, "You're killing me, Babe." He headed back into the shower, turned and looked at me, "You know you can always join me in there," he said winking.

He finished his shower and came back with just his boxers on. I got up shaking my head this time, "Nice shorts, wolfboy." I said walking passed him to take my shower.

He grabbed my wrist and pulled me into him kissing me, hard with hunger. I felt light headed and the heat in the pit of my stomach was on fire. I could get lost in his kiss alone.

He pulled his head back slightly smiling, "This way you'll think about me. While you're in there rubbing soap all over that great body of yours." He said between kisses.

I smiled and hit him in the back of the head, "You just love making this hard for me, don't you?"

"Again, ouch! Did you forget I just got the hell beat out of me?" he whined. I laughed and headed to the bathroom to take my shower. As I turned to go Chase smacked me on my butt, "Now we're even." He said with a smirk.

I got out of the shower and went out to the bedroom. Chase had dinner already done and was on the balcony. I walked out, and he smiled giving me a light kiss, saying, "I thought you might be hungry."

I smiled back at him, "I am, thanks. So is there anything you can't do?"

He just smiled, "When it comes to you, there's nothing I won't do."

I shook my head laughing, "You're so romantic and crap."

That made Chase laugh, "Why, thank you, babe I try."

We sat there eating and talked about the Ozarks and how he got two thousand acres. It was passed down to his dad and when his dad died of a heart condition, it was passed to Chase. I also found out that Chase was a carpenter. He helped his dad build this house.

When we were finally done and getting tired, I took the dishes downstairs, washed them and headed back up to bed.

Chase was already lying in bed, he smiled when I walked in. In a cunning voice he asked, "Do I get to cuddle with you tonight?"

I climbed into bed and moved close to him, "I don't know…maybe," I said smiling. He wrapped his arms around me and snuggled his face in my neck. He started kissing my neck up to my ear.

"You smell so good and I love seeing you wear my clothes," he whispered.

I reached down and took a hold of his hand, "I should smell good I used your soap. Your clothes, however, are too big on me, and since I have nothing on that belongs to me." I chuckled.

He flipped me over to face him. Putting himself over me with his arms at the side of my head so he could look me up and down, "What do you mean, you're not wearing *anything* of yours?" he said in low growl.

I pushed him back and turned to my side, "I've been here for two days and all my clothes are dirty. All of them," I said smiling.

He pulled me closer to him putting his face back to my neck, "You're killing me, Cady," he moaned as he continued kissing my neck and ear. I laughed, and we went to sleep....cuddling. I had a good dreamless night.

Fifteen

"Are you gonna sleep all day?" Chase said as he kissed my neck down to my collarbone and then back up my neck. It felt so good. I turned slightly to face him. I started went to say something, but, his lips found mine instantly. His kiss was passionate mixed with hunger, and he pulled me to where I was on top of him. His hands slid from the back of my neck down my back, stopping at my waist. I wrapped my fingers in his hair, pulling him into me harder. I was straddling his waist my body sliding up and down. It felt right and natural, like we could meld within each other.

"Morning," I said between kisses. Chase brought his hands up to my face, pulling my hair back away from my face and placing it on one side around my shoulder.

"Morning. What should we do this morning? I say we stay and do this all day." Chase said cunningly.

"Yeah, that would be nice and all, but, we really need to get going if we're going to make it back to Belton today," I said as I rolled off of him and started getting out of bed.

"Yeah, I know, but I still like my idea better," he said as he grabbed and pulled me back down next to him. I laughed as Chase rolled on top of me crushing my body under his. He brought his hand down and grabbed both of my hands, putting them over my head with one hand. He brought down his free hand to stroke the side of my face down my neck and back up to my lips. His hair hung down around my face, his bright green eyes never leaving mine. "Well, how about we just lay here for another....hour or two?"

I started laughing harder, "Yeah, that would be great, but we really do need to get going." I pushed him off of me and got out of bed. I turned and stared at him. He looked so good. His lip was almost healed, all the cuts were practically gone and his swollen face was healed. "Wow, you do heal fast," I said as I looked him over.

He shrugged, "I told you I did, and I also changed into my wolf form this morning and went hunting, while you were still sleeping. We heal faster that way."

"How long have you been up?" I asked.

He shrugged, "Only a couple hours."

"Is that why you look so good today, cause you changed into your wolf form? Nice," I said as I looked him and down. He jumped up out of bed and over to where I was in a blink of an eye.

I backed up against the wall, he pinned me to the wall with his body. His hands sliding up and down my sides, "So, you think I look good?" he said with a smile and raised brow. "Do you want to test out how much I've healed? Cause, I would love to show you." He said in a deep low voice.

I could feel the electricity flowing through both of us. I would love nothing more than to throw him back on the bed and see what he could really do. I just don't know if I'm ready or if my heart is ready for that yet. I have a feeling he could end up breaking my heart. I know I don't have to sleep with him to be his mate, but that would be like saying yes, in an unspoken way.

So I gave him a little push on his chest, "Come on, we got to get ready to leave. How many times do I have to remind you?" I asked, as I moved out of his grip and headed into the bathroom.

I was getting dressed in the bathroom when I heard a knock coming from the front door. I came out just as Chase was going to open the bathroom door, "Cady, stay up here." He said in a low voice.

I looked at him with my brow raised, "Are you on crack? I'm not staying up here while you go down there to see who it is. Unless there's a girlfriend you haven't told me about." I said as I crossed my arms over my chest.

"What? No, there's no girlfriend. I don't know who it is, but it could be the pack again and I don't want you getting hurt." He said in a low growl.

"Chase, I'm not some little damsel in distress. I know how to take care of myself, so knock your crap off right now." I said angrily.

He looked at me and relaxed his shoulders slightly. Taking my hand in hands, "Ok, I'm sorry. I just don't want anything to happen to you, I want to keep you safe and unbroken with me." He said with puppy looking eyes. He asked softly, "Will you at least stand behind me?" I raised my brow at that one. "Fine, stand beside me then?" He asked.

I rolled my eyes smiling, pulling him towards the door. "Can we talk about this later, when you're not so girly…..and yes I'll stand beside you."

He yanked me back to him, my back up against his chest. Sliding his hands around my waist and planting his face in my neck. In a low growl, "Mmm, I'll show how girly I am….later."

I just laughed, "Yeah, you know I still haven't decided about this mating thing…right?"

He tightens his grip around me and kissed my neck saying between kisses, "I'm just helping you out with making your decision." Someone knocked again.

I wiggled out of his grip, "Come on, someone apparently wants to talk to you." I said heading to the door.

We headed down the stairs hand in hand. When we got to the door, Chase took a deep breath opening the door and then looked over at me. There at the door with their heads down, stood the two jerks that held me while Chase was getting his ass kicked.

"What the hell do you asses want?" I asked furiously. Just then they looked up and they were pretty beat up.

Chase took one look at them and asked, "Oh shit, what happened to you guys?"

They both just looked down again, then one of them finally said, "We thought what Garrett did yesterday was wrong. So he told us to choose…man we're like brothers. So we told him we wanted out so…..so we are."

Chase stepped aside to let them in, "Come on in, let's get this shit figured out." As they walked in all I wanted to do was kick the crap out of them. I glanced over at Chase and gave him the 'what the hell look'. He just shrugs. Well this better be good.

"Cady, this is Nate, and his little brother, Avan. Guys this is, Cady." Chase said with nod of head.

"Hi, nice to meet you, Cady," Nate said with a slight smile. Nate looked about eighteen, black hair and blue eyes. He was about six foot tall with a cute face.

"Yeah, it's nice to meet you," Avan said. He looked like Nate's twin only slightly younger and a little shorter, maybe about 5'8.

I looked them both up and down, "Yeah, we met. Aren't you two the same jerks that held me down while your buddies tried to shatter Chase's body?" I asked crossly. They both put their heads down.

"Cady, be nice." Chase said smirking, "Let's at least hear what they have to say." He said coming over to stand next to me.

I looked at him with innocent eyes, "What, I am being nice. I didn't say or do what I wanted to. If I did I would have said, they were nothing but worthless pieces of shit and I'd love nothing more than to throw a lightning bolt up their asses."

I looked over at Nate and Avan, "But I didn't say or do any of that, did I?" I asked them. They both just shook their heads no. I smiled when I looked back at Chase, "See? I told you I was being nice."

He just laughed and kissed my cheek, "Well, then I guess you were being nice." He then looked at Nate and Avan asked, "So you didn't like what happened with me, and you got out. Now what are you guys going to do?"

They looked at each other then back at Chase. Nate said softly, "We were hoping we could join you and start a new pack?"

Chase looked over at me and asked, "What do you think?"

I thought about it for a minute and signed, "We could really use all the help we can get if we come across Eddie's dad. So I'm cool with it, if you are."

He then glanced back at Nate and Avan and asked, "I'm gonna let you know now, Cady is in any pack that I am. She comes with me. You guys cool with that?" They both nodded yes.

"Ok, well, I guess we're all heading to Belton, then." Chase said, "I'll go pack and load up the Jeep." Chase, Avan and Nate all went to help pack the Jeep with their stuff.

Since I had no clothes to pack, I went to the kitchen for some snacks to take. "Well, this trip will be, oh, so much fun," I muttered sarcastically to myself.

Sixteen

With all four of us loaded in Chase's Jeep, Chase drove and I sat in the front passenger's seat. Nate and Avan sat in the back. We pulled out onto the 71 highway, heading north. I looked over at Chase and asked, "Not to sound like some whining little girl or anything, but how long will it take to get to Belton?"

Chase reached over and put his hand on my thigh glancing at me saying, "I would say about three, maybe four hours. We'll get there as soon as we can, babe," As he left his hand on my thigh, I looked down and saw my hand was on top of his. I didn't remember putting it there.

I turned around in my seat, "So Nate, Avan, what do you all do? You know besides the whole werewolf thing." Nate laughed Avan just smirked.

Nate said, "I just got out of high school, and I'm still looking for the perfect job."

I laughed, "Aren't we all? Are you planning on going to college? If you don't mind me asking?"

"No, I don't mind at all, and yes, I plan on going to college. I want to be a teacher." He said smiling

"Oh, wow, that's impressive, that would be great to be a teacher."
I said.

Nate smiled, "Have you graduated yet?"

"I graduate this year, I also work at a little store. I sell mostly crystals and herbs, but Oma she's the owner, does readings and crap like that." I said.

"Wow, you go to school and work full time? Now that's impressive." Nate said smiling.

"My best friend Bani works there also. So we have a lot of fun most days. It really doesn't feel like work," I said smiling, thinking about Bani and all the wild crap we had done.

"So Avan, what do you do?" I asked trying to get him involved in the conversation.

He just stared out the window and mumbled, "I go to school." Well, isn't he just the great talker.

I simply said, "That's cool, do you just graduate this year?"

"Yeah," He didn't say anything else. He just kept staring out the window, looking bored.

Chase squeezed my thigh, I glanced over at him and he whispered, "He doesn't like to talk much to people he doesn't know. Don't take it personally." I nodded saying I understood.

"Cady, can I ask you something?" Nate asked.

I nodded and said, "Ask away."

"Well, I was just gonna ask… what the hell did you do to Vincent to piss him off enough to want you dead?" Nate asked quickly.

I looked at him puzzled, "Who the hell is Vincent?"

Chase looked in the rearview mirror and asked, "What do you know, Nate?"

Nate, looking confused said, "Vincent is Eddie's dad and all I heard was that he was after you and wanted you dead. That's what Garrett said anyway, but that's all he said." He softly said, "Well, he also said, not to help you, just let you die. He said no Valkyrie should live."

"I'm going to kill that guy," Chase growled through his teeth.

I huffed, "I wish he would quit telling people that I'm a Valkyrie, it's starting to piss me off." I took a deep breath and added, "But to answer your question, the reason Eddie's dad…. I mean Vincent is after me. Well that's because I killed Eddie, so I guess he's mad about it," I shrugged.

"Umm yeah, I would say he is. I overheard that Garrett called him and I figured they were talking about you, but the guy who told me didn't know who they were talking about," Nate said.

I turned and sat looking straight ahead towards the road. I softly said, "Yeah, well, he deserved it." Chase squeezed my thigh again, he knew it upset me. He knew I was thinking about Zane. As we drove, my mind drifted back to Zane. He had always been there to help, no matter what the problem was. Ever since the first day of grade three. That was the day we met.

He had come in the classroom, and put his books next to mine and Bani's. He gave us a big, wide smile and said, "Hi, I'm Zane. Is it ok if I sit with you guys?" We looked around and noticed all the other boys were sitting in the back. So why he wanted to sit with us was beyond me, until we got older and he told us he was gay. The day my parents disappeared, he ran the five miles from his house to mine. He came up to my room and found me curled up in my bed crying. He just laid down next to me and put his arms around me. He didn't say anything, just cried with me.

We drove in silence for a while, and I finally spoke up, "Are we going to stop anytime soon? I really have to pee and I'm hungry," I whined.

"There's a diner up the road a little ways, we'll stop there. Can you wait that long?" Chase said chuckling.

I rolled my eyes at him, "If I have to." That just made him and Nate both start chuckling. Avan still hadn't said anything. I decided, right then and there that I was gonna make that boy talk to me.

We finally pulled into a small town named, Ballard, Mo. It had one diner, pool hall and a small consignment shop, all on Main St. We pulled into the diner, got out of the car and walked in. Chase held the door open for me. As I passed him, he fell in right beside me, taking my hand. We all four walked to a table and the three guys went to sit down. I went to find a restroom. A few minutes later, as I came back to the table, I looked around, and I swear every woman in that place stopped what they were doing, and started gawking at the three guys sitting in the booth. Let's face it; they were three of the hottest guys I had ever seen. For one of them, you would sell your first born, just to be with him for five minutes, and he's the one who wants to be with me.

I started laughing, Chase looked over at me confused, "What's so funny, babe?" They were all three looking at me now with baffled faces.

I laughed harder, "Really? You guys don't notice anything different in this place?" They all started looking around the diner, and a few ladies smiled and waved.

Nate smiled slightly back, and then looked back at me, "I don't notice anything out of place. It looks normal to me," Nate said. Chase and Ian both nodded in agreement with Nate.

"Oh, my heavens!" I said throwing up my arms, "Every woman in this place is drooling all over you three, and they can't take their eyes off of you." They just kept staring at me like I had lost my mind, "Seriously, you guys don't see it at all?" All three shook their heads, no. "Hell, I just thought it was funny, but now you guys just worry me." I said shaking my head, still laughing.

All three looked around again. This time Avan started chuckling, "I see it." He leaned in towards me and whispered, "They're kinda scary looking though."

That got us both laughing, Chase and Nate both looked around again. They finally got it too. They started laughing and Chase moved his chair closer to me putting his arm around my shoulders. That got us all laughing even harder.

The waitress hurried over. She was in her mid-forties. She had red hair pulled back in a ponytail, her skirt was way too short and you could tell she had a boob job. "Can I get you anything, honey?" She asked Chase.

"Umm, sure, I'll have a number three, the burger and fries," Chase said.

"Sure thing sweetness, anything else?" she asked as she winked at Chase. He still had his arm around me. He took my hand in his and kissed it watching me the whole time. "What would you like, babe?" he asked.

I heard the waitress huff, I giggled, and "Number three sounds fine to me." Then I leaned into him and gave him long passionate kiss, "Mmm, but you taste so much better," I said in a seducing tone.

Avan pipe up raising his brow saying, "I'll have what he's having," Moving closer to me.

Nate put his hand on the table and I put my hand in his. "Me too," he said as he gazed into my eyes.

I looked up at the waitress, and said astutely, "We're all really close." The waitress huffed again and walked away. We all started laughing hard again. I looked to where she had walked to, then batted my eyes. "I hope it wasn't something we did," I said in my most innocent voice. That got all three of them laughing again.

Chase leaned over and whispered in my hair, "You're so mean."

I just smiled. "You started it."

Soon the food came and we all calmed down enough to eat. I guess we were just starving, or maybe tired of laughing so much. We finished eating, paid the bill and headed out the door with every woman still watching every move the men made.

As we pulled out of the parking lot, I heard this loud banging noise, "What the hell is that?" I asked loudly.

"Oh shit, everybody hold on!" Chase said, as the Jeep flew off the road in mid-air. I shut my eyes as tight as I could and held on to the 'oh shit' handle. I felt my insides roll with the Jeep over and over again. My head hit the window, and then flew back towards Chase. Chase tried to put his arm out to stop me from flying around, but he went flying back towards the window. The Jeep landed hard on the passenger side and slid to a stop.

Seventeen

As I was lying there, not wanting to move, my whole body started to hurt. I could feel the glass cutting into my back. I tried to look down to see if my body was still in one piece. I couldn't seem to move my head at all. Great, it probably got cut off and I'm laying here headless. I thought to myself.

I felt someone grab my hand, "Cady, are you ok?" Chase asked. He didn't sound too good, himself.

I moved my hand a little to make sure it still worked. "Yeah, I think so. Are you ok? How's Nate and Avan?" I asked in a low whisper.

It took him a minute to answer me, I thought maybe he didn't want to tell me something bad had happened to them. He finally answered, "They're both ok, I'm ok, but we need to get out of the Jeep. Can you move at all?"

I tried moving my legs, and yelled out in pain, "Umm, I think my legs are gone! I can't move them! Are they still on me?" I asked in a panic.

"Calm down, you still have your legs, but I think you're pinned." Chase said softly. "I'm going to try and lift the dash off of you, Cady. It might hurt a little, you ready?" Chase asked.

I was quiet preparing myself for the pain that I knew would come, "Oh great, that's just what I need, more pain! Yeah, I'm ready."

Chase took a grip on the dash and pulled as hard as he could. I could hear him grunting, trying to get it to move. It wasn't working, and then I saw Nate next to Chase trying to help him. It moved a little, but it didn't move enough for me to get my legs out.

"Ok, this isn't working," I said through clenched teeth. My legs were starting to hurt like the dickens, but I didn't want to say anything. "Maybe I can help." I said.

"No, I don't want you to move. Nate and I will try again, Avan will pull you out, once we have it up enough." Chase said.

"Chase, I can help and without moving! For heaven sakes I'm a witch, I don't need to move to make other things move." I said angrily. "Now, quit acting like a guy and move out of my way!"

"OK, ok sorry. What do you need us to do?" Chase asked. I could hear Nate chuckle and then grunt. Chase must've hit him.

I brought my hand up and flicked it just a little, the dash buckled and made a creaking noise. It started moving slowly up, "Ok, grab onto the dash so it doesn't fall back on me." I said. They both did what I said and Avan put his hands under my arms and pulled me out of the window.

I lay quiet for a moment, my body still hurting, but at least I could feel everything. I started to sit up slowly,

Chase came running over from around the jeep, "Baby, are you ok?"

"Am I alive?" I said sitting up. I looked around and saw the jeep. It had been totaled. How we all got out of there alive was beyond me.

"Yes, you're alive." Chase said smiling.

"Then I'm fine." I said. "What happened? Why did we go flying off the road?" I asked.

Chase looked around and then back at me, "I think some demons threw a fireball or something at us. All I really know is we need to get out of here, fast. Can you walk?"

I started to stand and felt a little shaky, so Chase grabbed my arm to help steady me. After I got my balance, I moved my arms and legs to make sure they still worked. I took my hand and put it on my head to make sure it was all good up there, too. When I finally comprehended I still had all my body parts and nothing was broken, I started stretching all my limbs.

Chase looked at me and smiled, "All good there?"

I smiled back, "All good."

"Good," Chase said as he wrapped his arms around my waist and pulled me closer to him. He brought his lips down to where they brushed against mine, "You had me worried, Babe." He didn't give me time to respond to him, he just crushed his lips to mine. I felt the electricity flowing between us. I opened my mouth, letting his tongue touch mine.

"I hate to break this up and all, but we really need to get moving. Those demons might be back any minute." Nate said.

Chase pulled his head back slightly, putting his forehead on mine, "Ok," he said to Nate

Chase released my waist and took a grip on my hand, "Let's get out of here." He said, as we started walking. I viewed the scenery as we walked, and there was nothing to look at. There were fields with cows on one side and woods on the other side with a gravel road between them.

I heard a low noise and as I turned to see what it was, Chase pushed me to the ground, "Get down," he yelled as he got on top of me. I looked over his shoulder and saw about ten demons shooting fireballs at us. Chase rolled one way and I another, and they barely missed us. All four of us scrambled up and ran into the woods. The demons ran after us. I got behind a tree and stopped. I looked to see how far away the demons were, they were about fifty feet away. I needed to move fast if I wanted to surprise them.

Someone grabbed my wrist, I jumped back and went to kick him, but noticed it was Avan at the very last second. "What are doing, Cady? You need to keep running." He whispered loudly.

"I'm thinking, you guys go and hide behind some trees. I'm gonna take out some demons on this end. I need to make sure you guys watch my back, so no demons can sneak up on me." I said.

Just then Chase must've realized I wasn't right behind him, because he came running over to where Avan and I were. "What the hell, we need to keep moving." He also whispered loudly.

"You can't outrun demons Chase, trust me I know how they work. We have to surprise them and we don't have time to argue about this. Now get behind some damn trees and let me do what I do best!" I whispered just as loudly, "And that's dealing with demons!"

"Ok, I'll be right here if you need me then." Chase said worriedly.

I smiled, "Thank you, for trusting me, Chase."

He gave me a quick kiss on the lips, "I'll always trust you. We'll do this together, no macho wolf here. I think you can do whatever we do, if not better." He said winking.

I ran over to another tree and stood behind it. The demons were about thirty feet now. It's now or never I thought. I walked out from behind the tree, so the demons could see me. It didn't take them long to notice me, and they all stopped dead in their tracks. One of them walked to the front.

"Well, well, it looks like your friends left you behind, little girl." he said in a crude tone. I just stood there, with my hands behind my back, both dripping off frost and electricity, just waiting.

"No, I decided to stop and take in the scenery and maybe go cow tippin. I always wanted to try that." I said sweetly.

That made them all laugh, the demon said, "Oh little girl, you should have ran with your friends." He spread his arms wide, smiling, "You see, now you're going to die and we all are going to take our time doing it. You will suffer for quite some time before we finally kill you. You'll be begging us by the end to kill you and get it over with."

I smiled, "Now, see that's where you're wrong...I don't beg for anything, and I won't be the one dying today. That, my friend, will be you." I said, as I brought my hand up and shot a lightning bolt at them. They all dove out of the way, so I shot another, this time hitting one of them in the arm.

"What the hell, you're a witch!" one of them yelled. They shot some fireballs at me, I moved behind the tree.

"What did you think I was? Some little defenseless human girl, that couldn't defend myself?" I yelled back at them from behind the tree. I threw a few ice balls towards them and they jumped out of the way again.

"That's ok, we've killed plenty of witches before you. You'll just add to our collection," One of them yelled.

A few more fireballs flew by my head. I looked over and saw Chase staring at me with worried eyes.

I looked from behind the tree and they were getting closer. Crap, I needed to figure out how I was going to kill them. I eyed two of them standing side by side and not paying any attention to where I was. I shot a lightning bolt and an ice ball at them, hitting them both in the chest. Both fell to the ground, hopefully dead.

The rest of the demons ran, throwing fireballs towards me the whole time. All I could do was hide behind the tree, so I wouldn't get hit. One of them got close enough to where Chase jumped out, grabbed him and broke his neck.

The tree caught on fire and began to break apart. I dove out of the way of a falling limb. I was now cut off from Chase by the fire. Oh great, now what am I gonna do? I thought to myself. I had five demons running towards me, still throwing fireballs at me. I turned and ran the other way through the woods.

I ran over limbs that had fallen and under branches hanging low. I could feel the heat from the fire, so I shot out some frost towards the fire while I ran, trying to put it out. I slowed down enough to look behind me to see if they were still chasing me. One still was, and he was gaining on me fast. He shot a fireball that barely missed my head. I fell to the ground when I went to get back up, I felt something on my back.

"Where you going little girl?" the demon asked as he pushed harder on my back with his foot.

"Oh, you know, just going for a nice little run through the woods." I said trying to get up again. He again pushed me back down.

He took his foot off my back, good. Maybe I can scramble up now and get away. I started to get up and he kicked me in my side. I went flying into a tree, hitting my shoulder. He came at me again, "I'm gonna enjoy this." He said cockily.

I smiled, "Me too," I said as I threw a lightning bolt into his chest. He fell over dead. I jumped up and ran as hard as I could. I didn't know where I was going, but I knew where ever I ended up Chase would be able to track me.

Eighteen

I ran until I finally came out of the woods into a field. In the middle of it stood an old abandoned looking mansion. "Wow, now that house is huge." I muttered to myself. It was four stories high, white with blue shutters. It used to be a beautiful house, if someone had taken care of it, but now it looked old and worn. As I walked up to the mansion, I noticed crystals lying around the house. "This is a scary movie just waiting to happen." I said, as I walked up to the door.

As I walked up onto the porch, I could hear the creaking under my feet. I came to the door, and reached my hand up to knock on the door. I grabbed the doorknob, turning the handle and the door opened. Slowly I stepped through the door. "Hello, is anyone here?" I called out. Slowly I walked inside and looked around. What I saw was amazing. The foyer was huge with pillars in each corner.

There was a staircase spiraling up on both the left and right side of the room. There was a door on the left and three doors on the right. "Great, it's gonna be like walking through a maze," I muttered to myself.

I went over to the door on the left and slowly opened it up. As I walked in, I saw a big room full of old tables and chairs. Wow, I thought, this is like a big ballroom, I'm just waiting to see a princess walk in. I looked around for a while longer and decided there was nothing in this room that could help me.

As I walked out of the room, I heard a noise coming from one of the rooms on the other side of the foyer. I slowly walked over to one of the doors, and put my ear to the door to see if I could hear anything in this one. I didn't, so I went to another door, and listened, "Shhh, she might hear us," someone said through the door.

"Well, then, get off me, you're crushin' my foot." Someone else said. They sound younger than me. I lifted my hand up in case I needed to freeze them, and slammed into the door, pushing it open.

The kids went scrambling backwards, trying to get up and out of the way. I stopped in mid stride, "What the …. How old are you guys?"

One boy stood up and walked forward, saying, "I'm sixteen and fine, so you better leave." He was about 6'0 feet tall with black hair, and pale green eyes.

"Listen, as much as I would love to leave, I can't. I have about six guys after me." I said harshly.

Another guy stepped up and held his hand out, "I'm Brad," he said. He was about 5'8, sandy brown hair and blue eyes, and really cute.

I held my hand out and shook his hand, "I'm Cady," I said smiling.

"So Cady, how come the demons are after you?" Brad asked.

"Why do you say demons? I said guys were after me." I asked raising my brow.

He just laughed, "Cause, demons are always after someone. That's why we are here and the crystals are outside. They protect the house so they can't get in."

"Don't tell her anything. We don't know her. She could just be some girl." The other guy said in a hushed voice.

"I'm a witch, and yeah, demons are after me. I just don't know *why* they're after me." I said eyeing the other guy.

Brad looked at the other guy and then back at me, "That's Cooper, and he's a little paranoid… you said six demons? There's usually about ten of them at a time." Brad said.

"I took three of them out, and a friend of mine got another one that I know of. I don't know what happened to the rest. Hopefully, my friends took out the rest of them." I said.

Brad smiled, "Well, you can stay here as long as you want to. This place has been abandoned for a long time, so no one will look for you here."

"Thanks, so you guys are warlocks?" I asked. I can tell the different types of Supernatural's, expect for other witches and warlocks. So that's what they must be.

Brad smiled again, "Yup, Cooper and I are warlocks and there are three girls with us that are witches. Come on, I'll show you around and introduce you to the others."

I followed Brad and Cooper up the stairs to another room, as we walked in I saw three girls huddled in the corner holding each other. "It's ok guys, you can get up now. She's not here to kill us. The demons are after her." Cooper said.

All three girls got up and walked over to where I was standing, "Hi, I'm Violet, and this is Brit and Kate."

The girls shook my hand, "Hi, I'm Cady." Violet was a short girl with long brown hair and hazel eyes. The other two looked like twins, both had short blond hair with brown eyes. "How long have you been here?" I asked Violet.

"About five months, I think. After the demons burnt down our orphanage." She said looking down.

Oh wow, they're all orphans, and I thought I had it bad. "So how old are you guys, if you don't mind me asking?" I asked them all.

Brad walked over to where I was. "Cooper and I are seventeen, Violet is sixteen and the twins are fourteen. We take care of each other. So Cady, how old are you?"

"I just turned eighteen, I'm trying to get back home, but the demons crashed the car we were in." I said. I looked at Brad, he smiled even more. I slightly smiled back, wondering where Chase was and hoping he was ok.

"There's an old jeep in the back, but it doesn't run." Brad said.

I smiled, "If I can get it to run, can I borrow it to get back home?" I asked.

"Sure, you can have it, if you know anything about cars." Cooper said sarcastically.

"I know a little about them, I rebuilt my Mustang." I said just as sarcastically. He just huffed and walked to the corner with his arms folded crossed his chest. I just chuckled.

It was getting dark outside. I kept looking out the window but still no sign of Chase. I was starting to get worried. "Are you hungry?" Violet asked.

"No, thank you," I said.

"Ok, well, if you want, I'll take you to one of the rooms you can sleep in." Violet said.

"Thanks that would be nice. I am getting a little tired." I said walking over to the door with her.

"We're gonna go check out the other rooms for Cady." Violet told the others. "You can stay in my room, Cady," Brad said smiling.

"Umm thanks, but I don't think so." I said wrinkling my brow.

He just shrugged, "Ok, just trying to help."

As we walked down the hall I asked, "So how many rooms are in this place?"

She looked over at and said, "There's twenty bedrooms with a bathroom in each, a huge kitchen, a big ballroom, a family room and the main bathroom. I'm sure there other rooms also, but, we just haven't seen all of them yet. Luckily for us there's a well outside with water in it." We went to one the rooms and Violet opened the door. "You can have this one, it's next to mine in case you need anything. You'll have to clean it up a little, sorry."

I looked around the room and was amazed by how large the room was. The only thing in the room was a bed, on the floor covered in dust. "Thanks, it looks great." I said.

As I started cleaning the dust off the bed, Violet came over and started helping me. We got the bed clean and Violet went over to a closet and grabbed some blankets. We took them out to the balcony and shook off all the dust on them, then we made the bed. I smiled, "There. All good, thanks for helping me Violet."

She smiled back, "No problem," she said as she walked over to the door, she stopped and looked over, "I hope your friends are ok."

Smiling back at her I said, "Thanks, me too."

I sat down on the bed and thought about Chase. I hope he's ok, with the fire and the demons. I laid my head down, still thinking about him, wondering where he was.

I must've doze off, because the next thing I knew, I sat straight up in bed. I listened, thinking I had heard something. There was a loud banging noise. I jumped out of bed and ran over to the door, as soon as I opened it I ran into Brad.

"What was that?" I asked.

"I have no idea, it's coming from the door though. Whoever it is can't come in, the house is protected against everything except witches and warlocks." Brad said as we ran down the stairs.

The banging was coming from the front door, "I'll break the damn thing down!" I heard Chase say beyond the door.

I ran over to open the door while all the kids behind me yelled, "No!! Cady, what are doing! Run!" I don't know who said what. All I cared about what was behind that door.

I opened and Chase was standing there, getting ready to bang on the door again. He saw me, dropped his hand and I ran out and he picked me up hugging me tight,

"Cady, are you ok?" Chase whispered in my ear as he held me tight.

"I'm fine. What took you so long?" I asked smiling.

"You know, just strolling the woods, taking in the scenery and seeing what we could find." Chase said, with his arms still wrapped around my waist.

I laughed, "So how many did you guys end up getting?" I asked.

"Only two, the rest ran. I wanted to find you, so I let them run," Chase shrugged. I flicked my wrist to move one of the crystals, so they all could come in the house.

"Oh my, you guys killed two demons?" Violet asked excitedly.

"Yeah, but I think there are four more. They might try and come back. Sorry." Nate said.

I looked over at Nate and Avan, smiled at both of them and said, "Are you two ok?"

Nate smiled, "Just fine Cady." Avan had his head down,

I walked over to him and took his chin in my hand to lift up his head. He had a long cut over his eye, "Oh my heavens, Avan what happened?" I asked worriedly.

He tried to look down again, but I wouldn't let him. "I'm fine, just got cut, that's all." He said shrugging.

I shook my head, "Let's go get it cleaned up a little. You look gross."

He slightly smiled, "Ok." Violet walked over to where I was standing.

"Cady, I'll take him and get the cut cleaned up." she said smiling at Avan.

He smiled back at her, "Thanks." He said shyly.

We all went into the family room and I introduced everyone. "These guys helped me out, this is Brad, Cooper, Violet and the twins Brit and Kate. Everyone, these are the friends I was telling you about, Chase, Avan and Nate."

Everyone said their hellos, Chase gave me an odd look. Cooper actually smiled, but Brad on the other hand kept giving Chase dirty looks. Avan and Violet stood over in the corner talking, while Nate played with the twins. It was getting pretty late and I was getting tired. "There's an old Jeep out in the back, and they said we could use it, if I can get it to run." I told Chase.

He raised his brow, "You know how to fix cars?"

I smiled, "Yes I do. There's a lot that you don't know about me."

Chase looked down and quietly said, "No, I guess I don't." Brad again gave him a dirty look and Chase gave a low growl that no one could here but me. I looked between the both of them confused.

We all headed up to bed, Nate and Avan took the room next to Violet and Chase and I were on the other side of her room. I lay down on the bed, Chase walked in after me, "Friends? Is that what we are, just friends?"

I looked at him puzzled, "What are you talking about?"

He sat on the side of the bed and looked at me with sad eyes, "You introduced me as your friend. Is that all I am to you? Should I be jealous of that Brad, guy?"

I looked at him confused, "I honestly don't have a clue in what you're talking about."

His head was down, "I saw the way he was looking at you. I know I can't call you mine until you say, but I thought I was more than just a friend. So should I be worried?"

I sat up next to him, and quietly said, "No, you shouldn't be worried, and yes you are more than a friend. Sorry I didn't mean for it to sound like that. I don't know…I don't know what you want me to call you?"

He wrapped his arms around me. "What would you like us to be? You know what I want, the question is, what do you want us to be?"

I laid my head on his chest, "Can we talk about this later? I'm really tired." He didn't say a word. We went to sleep not saying anything else, just holding each other.

Suddenly, there was a loud bang that shook the entire house. We both jumped up and out of bed, "What the hell was that?" I asked.

Nineteen

I ran over to the window and looked out, "Oh great, it's those damn demons!" I yelled at Chase.

He was beside me at the window, "Great, what do you want to do?" he asked me.

I looked over at him and smiled, "Let's get rid of them once and for all. There's only four of them."

We ran out of the room, and Nate and Avan met us in the hallway, "What the hell was that?" Nate asked.

Soon everyone was out in the hallway, so I told everyone, "It's the demons we ran into earlier." I looked over at Brad and Cooper, "What's your main power?" They both looked down, so I looked over at Violet. She also had her head down. "Do you guys know your main power?" I asked them all. They all shook their head no, well, crap! I thought.

"Ok, later we're gonna have to work on your powers, but for now I guess I can handle it." I said.

Chase came over to where I was, "Where do you want us?" he said pointing at himself, Nate and Avan. I stood there thinking about what the hell to do. Four demons were outside wanting to fry us, but they couldn't get in due to the crystals around the house.

"Ok, what if I go out there and shoot some lightning bolts at them, and you guys sneak up behind them?" I asked.

Chase raised his brow, "No,"

I looked over at him, "And why not?"

Chase walked over to me, "Because I said so that's why not. You're not putting yourself in danger on purpose."

I put my hands on my hips, "I'm sorry, but did you just say, because you said so? Cause, I think you better be coming up with something else a little better than that crap!"

He took a hold of my hand, "Excuse us, we need to go talk for a minute." Brad snickered as we walked by, Chase growled and Brad looked away quickly. We went into the kitchen and Chase slammed the door behind him.

We stood there glaring at each other, until finally Chase broke eye contact. "Cady, why do you always have to be the first one to put yourself in the middle of danger?" he asked as he walked over to me.

I put my hands on my hips, "I'm not always putting myself in danger, Chase. Do you have a better plan? Cause I'm all for another plan," I said backing away as he tried to take my hand.

He stopped trying to take my hand and sat down on a stool. He looked defeated, but I didn't care. He had pissed me off, trying to tell me what to do. His head hung down. "Cady, you don't get it." He said quietly.

"Then explain to me what I don't get!" I said angrily.

He finally looked up at me, and I could see the anger and frustration in his eyes. He jumped right in front of me, making me jump, back against the wall. He came inches from my face, "Fine, you want me to explain it to you!" he growled, "Cady, I don't want anything to happen to you. So, if trying to keep you safe, makes *me* look like some big ass jerk, then so be it. I'd rather be a jerk and you alive, then keep my mouth shut and you dead. Damn it, Cady, I love you!" he yelled.

I stared at him wide eyed. I quietly asked, "You love me?"

He never took his eyes off of me. "Yes, I love you. I know you need time and all to figure out what you want, but this is how I feel. I don't expect you to say it back or anything. I just...I just needed to tell you how I felt and why I'm so against you putting yourself in danger all the time. I don't want to lose you, Cady," he said quietly.

I stood there, not knowing what to do or think. How did I feel? I didn't think I wanted to lose him, and I was worried when I didn't know where he was, but do I love him? I gazed into his beautiful emerald green eyes, I took a hold of his hand, "I...I don't know what to say? I know I don't want to lose you either, but I just...I. Man, I suck at this, I..."

Chase grabbed me wrapping me in his arms, kissing me passionately. He pulled back slightly, "I'm not asking you to say anything. I'm just trying to explain. I'll be honest with you, I get scared when you take all these chances and put yourself in danger."

"I understand that, I do. Fine, what do you suggest we do then?" I asked quietly.

He kissed my forehead, "You know I'll do whatever you want me to do, and if that's you going out there fighting. I'll be right there with you. I just had to put my two cents in about how I felt. That's all."

I smiled, "That's all I ask." I put my arms around his neck. "So, we do this together? You, not trying to put me behind you?"

His arms still wrapped around my waist, pulled me closer, "Whatever you say, I'll do." He said as he kissed me again.

We walked out to the family room, and everyone stared at us as we walked in, "Ok, this is what we're gonna do, Nate and Avan go with Chase. You guys are gonna go out the back door, change into your wolf form thing. I'm gonna go out the front door and distract them, then you attack from behind, ok?" I said to Nate and Avan.

Brad came up, "What about us, what are we supposed to do?" Brad asked.

"None of you know what your main witch power is, but you guys do have some powers, right?" I asked.

Violet came over and stood by Brad, "Yeah, we can make fog and make things look invisible." Violet said. I thought about what Violet just said.

It was easy to make fog and to become invisible, but I wasn't going to tell them that, "Ok, that's good, that just might be able to help us." As we all sat down and talked about the plan, we could hear the demons still outside throwing fireballs at the house. Soon they would break through the crystals, so we had to hurry. After we made the plan, Chase came over to me.

"Please be careful," He said as he kissed my forehead.

I smiled, "You too, wolfboy," I said.

I went to the front door and waited. I had told Chase I would wait ten minutes before I went out. That would give him time to change and get into place. Brad, Violet and Cooper went to the second floor window just above the front door. The twins stayed downstairs, hiding in one of the bathrooms. I waited the ten minutes and walked out of the front door.

As soon as the door shut behind me, the four demons all looked my way. I smiled, "Well, hey there boys! How's your night goin so far?"

One of them stepped up and smiled a wicked smile, "It's about to get a lot better." As soon as the words came out of his mouth, he shot a fireball at me. I dove out of the way, standing back up I gave him a dirty look.

"Well, now that's just rude, and here I was trying to be nice." I said as I threw out a few ice balls at them, and they all ducked out of the way.

Violet, Brad and Cooper made the fog come rolling in, and it came up to my knees. The demons looked around worriedly. "What the hell is this?" one of them asked. I had a tingle in my chest, but I pushed it down. I looked over and I saw three wolves come around the corner of the house.

There was the most beautiful animal that I've ever seen, and no doubt in my mind of which one it was. Chase, I thought. He stood double in height of a regular wolf, with a nice golden blond coat and his bright emerald green eyes shining, as he looked at me. The demons didn't see them. I shot a lightning bolt at them.

The demons dodged and tried to throw fireballs at me, but I became invisible at the same time. They stopped mid fire and looked around. The only bad thing about becoming invisible is that it only lasts about ten seconds. I did a summersault towards a tree, with the demons to my left. I became visible I yelled, "Hey!" They all turned to look at me, and I held up my middle finger and smiled, becoming invisible again.

The three wolves jumped out from behind and each one grabbed a demon. The one left came towards me, throwing fireballs as he moved closer. I froze his fire and shot out a lightning bolt at the same time, hitting him in the chest. He burst into flames, falling to the ground.

Chase had one of the demons by the neck, throwing him against a tree, and snapped his neck. The other two weren't far behind, Nate ripped out number two demon's throat. Avan, on the other hand, looked like he was playing with his demon. He had the demon by the neck shaking him and tossing him in the air, then catching him in his mouth. As he came back down, he shook him again. This time as he threw him in the air, he caught him and ripped out his neck. Two of the wolves went around the house and disappeared. Chase came up to where I was and put his nose on my hand. I was almost face to face with him.

He was a lot bigger up close, I put my arm around his neck, "Nice going, wolfboy," I said smiling. He gave a low growl, almost like he was laughing. He then turned and disappeared around the corner of the house with the other two. I turned and walked into the house.

Brad, Violet and Cooper all came running down the stairs, "You did it, you killed those demons!" Violet yelled as she ran up to me.

"No, we all did it. It took everyone working together to kill them. So nice jobs guys, the fog and turning me invisible worked great!" I said excitedly. Just then the guys came in from outside, luckily all wearing clothes and the twins came out of the closet.

The twins ran up and both of them hugging me, "Thank you so much. If you guys wouldn't have showed up, those demons would still be trying to get us." Kate said. I just smiled, I never was good with praise.

"Maybe we should all head to bed, it's about two in the morning, and you have a Jeep to fix tomorrow." Chase said to me as he took my hand. We all said goodnight and headed to the rooms we were staying in.

Twenty

I was standing in a field full of flowers watching myself with Chase. He was standing behind the other me, "Its ok, you don't have to try if you don't want to." Chase whispered in my ear.

His arms were wrapped around my waist, I took hold of his hands, "No, I want to do it, I want to do it with you," The other me said.

He smiled and kissed my neck, "Ok, whenever you're ready then." The other me walked a few steps in front of Chase and stopped. I turned around and smiled, there was pure love in my eyes as I gazed at Chase. I felt a little jealous. Did I look at him like that at all? I wondered to myself.

The other me started taking her shirt off, then her pants and finally her under clothes. Chase did the same.

Great I don't want to stand here and watch her, well, me have sex with Chase. That doesn't seem right, somehow.

Oh hell, it's like a train wreck, you want to look away, but can't. As I continued to watch them, neither were moving. "Just relax and let it happen. Trust me," Chase said.

The other me nodded her head, "I trust you." the other me said. Ok, now it must be a dream because I don't trust anybody but three people and he's not one of them.

All of a sudden the other me fell to her knees, Chase did the same. The other me began screaming out in pain. What the hell is going on? I wondered to myself. Hair started spouting out of every pore of their bodies, I could hear the cracks and breaks of their bones. They both were now on all fours with their heads down. After what seemed like hours, but merely minutes they both looked up at the same time. They were both wolves! The other me had a blond coat with a red tint to it, and had the same teal with gold streaked eyes I have. Chase walked slowly over to the other me and hit her with his nose. The other me hit him back with her nose, and then they ran off into the woods. They almost sounded like they were laughing. They were also jumping on and off of each other, growling and nipping at each other.

I sat straight up in bed, Oh, my heavens! I looked over at Chase; he was still sleeping. Ok, it was just a dream, I said to myself. I laid there thinking about the weird dreams I've been having lately. What the hell is happening to me? I got up quietly and went to the balcony, and as I looked over, I could see the sun was just starting to come up. It was beautiful with all the colors coming through the trees and on to the ground. I heard Chase come out on to the balcony behind me. "How long have you been up?" Chase asked as he put his arms around my waist.

I took a long deep breath in, "Just for a little while, I wanted to think." I said.

"Is everything ok?" he asked. I stood there and thought about it for a while. And I decided right then all I wanted to do was go home.

"No, I really just want to go home." I said hoping he would just leave it at that. Chase was quite for a minute before he finally asked what I was hoping he wouldn't.

"Cady, when you get home and make sure your friends are ok, you are still leaving and coming back with me?" Chase asked. I turned around so I could face him. It was so hard to say anything when I looked up into his beautiful green eyes.

"Chase, I can't just leave them. I know I told I would, but I can't." I said. I still couldn't look him in the eyes. So I just hung my head down.

"Cady, look at me," Chase said as he took a hold of my chin in his hand and make me look up. "I know you want to go home and I know it will be hard for you to leave again, but you're not safe there right now. If it will make you feel better, bring your friend with you."

"Chase, how do you know what you want?" I asked.

Chase looked deep into my eyes and smiled, "I know I want you and I want you happy and safe."

"How do you know for sure you want me? I asked. "You really don't know me. All you know about me is what you've seen these past few days, and all you have seen was me lose one of my best friends, and worry about the other. Oh, and let's not forget the fact that you saw me kill my ex-boyfriend." I said. All I could think about, was that one of us is going to get hurt. That someone will probably end up being me.

"Cady, when I…" I held up my hand to make him stop talking.

"No, really Chase, you know nothing about me." I said as I wiggled out of his grip and walked back inside. I needed him as far away as possible right now. "I mean really, did you know I hate cooking? I don't like to get all dolled up and go out partying. I like wearing my hair in a ponytail instead of letting it hang down. I suck at relationships, I'm either pushing guys away or screwin it up somehow." I was ranting like a crack head, but I couldn't stop myself. I needed to get it all out or I was gonna chicken out of what I was saying. I finally looked over at Chase and he was just standing there leaning up against the doorframe with his arms folded over his chest.

"I don't think this is a good idea. The you and me thing. You know what you think you want and I think you're wrong. So why don't we just stop it all before someone gets hurt?" I said quickly.

Chase pushed himself off the door frame and was in front of me in two strides. I backed up against the wall and he kept coming. He was inches from my face, his hands were on the wall blocking me from moving. "You want to know what I think, Cady? I think you are so scared of being hurt that you won't give anyone a chance to get close to you. When I look at you all I see is how you don't trust anyone and god forbid you let anyone in to help you or anyone that just wants to be with you." Chase said.

I was shocked. No one had ever talked to me like that, and I wasn't not about to let him start. "Hey…" I started to say.

"No, you had your turn, now it's mine. I knew the first time I looked into your eyes that you were meant for me. Call it a wolf thing, call it whatever you want, but I saw it clearly. I saw us growing old together, I saw always being together. Hell, I saw how stubborn you are, how insecure you are and how you won't let people in and you don't trust them. I saw it all, and I knew how hard it was gonna be to get you to trust me and let me in, and I still wanted to be with you, but until you see too… there's not much else to say. You'll always wonder, so I'll just wait till you figure out what you want. When you do let me know."

Chase said has he walked out the door, slamming it behind him.

"Well I guess I just screwed that up." I said to myself as I walked back to the balcony, I really hadn't intended to start a fight. I just wanted to know how he was so sure he wanted me, that's all. My head was just so over whelmed with everything that's going on, I'm worried about Bani and Oma, I'm still upset about Zane and now Vincent is gonna want me dead after he finds out about Eddie. Now Chase hates me. Can my life suck anymore?

There was a knock on the door. I thought it might be Chase coming back to apologize or at least say what a dumbass I was being….again. I went over to open the door, Brad stood at the door smiling, "Hi, can I come in?" Brad asked.

It took me a minute to realize it wasn't Chase like I was hoping. "Umm, sure," I said. I opened the door wider and he walked in.

"So, what's up?" I asked. He stood there with his hands in his pockets looking down at the floor.

Finally he looked up and smiled, "Well you said you were trying to get back to your home town to make sure everyone was ok. Right?"

"Yeah, some crap happened and I want to make sure they're all right. I would just call, but I don't have my phone with me." I said. He reached deeper in his pocket and pulled out an old looking cell phone. It looked like one of those prepaid kind.

"Well, it just so happens I have a phone, if you want to call and check on them?" he said still smiling like he won a World Series or something.

I slightly smiled back, "Thanks, but I can't remember their numbers. They were all programmed in my phone and all I had to do was look up their name." I said thinking I should've paid more attention to the numbers, instead of the names. Damn technology.

"I kinda have a spell that can get you to remember the numbers, as long as you were the one that programmed into your phone?" Brad said. I thought about when was the last time I programmed my phone and it was right after I dumped Eddie. He wouldn't leave me alone and wouldn't quit texting and calling me so I had to change my number. I had to reprogram all my numbers again.

"Yeah, I programmed them all myself." I said.

Brad smiled, "Good, you ready to start then?" I nodded and we both sat down on the floor in front of the bed. Brad held his hand out to me and I took them into mine.

"So where did you learn this spell? It's a pretty hard spell to master, Brad." I asked.

"I knew a guy, and he showed me what to do. He lived at the orphanage with me, but he didn't make it out alive." Brad said. He was looking everywhere but at me, so I assume he didn't want to talk about it.

"Ok, let's do this." I said. I was so ready to remember Bani's number. I just want to make sure she was ok, and that Vincent didn't hurt her somehow.

We sat down on the floor in the middle of the room, our legs crossed, and palms on our knees. Brad grabbed two candles and sat them beside us. "Ok, we have to hold hands." Brad said has he lit the candles.

"Ok," I said taking his hands into mine. "So, now what do we do?" I asked.

Brad squeezed my hands, smiling, "All you have to do is concentrate about the last time you put the number in. I'll do the rest."

I started thinking about the time I put the numbers in, and luckily Bani's was the first number. I remember sitting on my bed at home with my new phone in one hand and my old one in the other. I took out the sim card and put it in my new phone, but none of the numbers were on it. So I started programming all my numbers by hand. As I was trying to think about the numbers I put in, I could hear Brad chanting, but it sounded far away. I started focusing harder on the phone numbers I was putting in my new phone. I could suddenly see Bani's name and her number. I could see it like it was right in front of me! I needed to write it down as quickly as possible so I wouldn't forget. I concentrated deeply not to forget the number. I could see it clearly like it was right in front of me. I felt Brad let go of my hand, and put something in it. It felt like a pen, so while I was still concentrating on the number, I put my hand down and began to write. When I was done, I opened my eyes and looked down. Bani's number was there. I remembered it, so finally I could call and make sure she was ok. I jumped with the number clutched in my hand, and Brad stood up also.

I threw my arms around him saying, "Thank you. Thank you so much! I don't know how I can ever repay you!" I said happily. As I was still hugging Brad the door open and Chase walked in.

"I forgot my shirt…" Chase said as he trailed off as soon as he saw us hugging. I let go of Brad and looked at Chase, and the look on his face was nothing but hurt and sadness.

"Chase, Brad was helping me find…" I started to say.

Chase cut me off, "I'm sure he was helping you out a lot, but it's none of my business what you do."

Chase grabbed his shirt and walked out, slamming the door behind him. "So you two fighting or something?" Brad asked. I looked down at the number in my hand and then back at Brad.

"It doesn't matter right now, I need to get a hold of my friend. Thanks again for helping me." I said.

Brad handed me his phone and started walking towards the door, "Good luck. I hope you contact your friend and she's ok." As he opened the door to walk out he stopped and turned to look at me, "And I'm sorry if I messed up things with you and Chase."

I smiled, "You didn't do anything, I did it all. But thanks again for the help." Brad smiled back and walked out the door, closing it behind him.

Twenty-one

I sat down on my bed, the phone still in my hand. I was nervous. She better be ok. Or Vincent is dead. I dialed the number and waited.

"Hello." Bani said on the other end.

"Oh my heavens! Bani. Are you ok?" I asked. There was silence on the other end, I hope she didn't hang up.

"Cady, oh my... is that you? Where have you been? Are you ok? Where are now? What did you do? What happened that night at the club?" Bani kept talking so fast.

"Bani! Slow down, I'll tell you everything, I just need to know you're ok first." I said trying to get her to hear me and quit talking.

"Ok, I'm listening, but it better be good!" Bani said.

I sat there for a minute trying to figure out what to say, "I don't know where to start, but first I want to make sure you're ok?" I asked.

"Yes, I'm fine. Now tell me what's goin on!" Bani said a little harshly. I chuckled, that's Bani, straight to the point.

"Ok, it's a long story, but here I go…" I told her what happened at of the club after she left; we both cried when I told her about Zane and how I killed Eddie. "I'm so sorry Bani, I really did try to stop them, but somehow he blocked my powers." I said still crying.

"Cady, it wasn't your fault, so quit blaming yourself. It was Eddie not you." Bani said. We continued talking about everything that went on that night.

I finally started telling Bani about Chase and the mating thing, "I think I screwed it all up though, Bani. He's a great guy and all, but the whole mating thing... I was kinda scared, you know how I get, and I was so worried about you and Oma…"

"What. Let me get this right," Bani said interrupting me. "This guy literally told you that you two were meant to be together and you walk away from that?"

"No, I didn't walk away...I just don't know what to do. I don't want to get hurt." I said quietly.

"Awe Cady, you never know until you try it. Just give it a chance. Now change of subject. Where are you? Cuz I'm coming to you." Bani said.

"I'm in a little town called Ballard, but I'm kinda hiding out in an abandon mansion type place. I don't know how long I can stay here." I said.

Bani started laughing, "Damn girl, just go down to the bank and buy the place. You got the money to do it. Besides if you say Vincent is after you, it won't be long' till he comes looking for me or Oma. So, I should bring her too, you think?"

"Yeah, that would be great, at least I would know you're both safe." I said, "How long do you think it will take you guys to get here?" I asked.

"Give me a couple days to get ready and find the place. But we will be there, so have a cool room waiting for me." Bani said laughing.

"I will," I said laughing. I gave her directions and we said our goodbyes as I hung up the phone. Knowing Bani and Oma were safe, it felt like the world was lifted off my shoulders. If only it could be that simple with Chase.

I walked out of the bedroom looking for Brad to give him his phone back, "Hey, Violet, have you seen Brad?" I asked.

"I think he's outside getting all the tools out for you to fix that jeep." Violet said.

"Ok, thanks," I said as I headed towards the door. I walked outside and over the six car, garage, I opened the door and stopped. I could hear people in the garage talking, so I put my ear up to the door to listen.

"Dude, I just don't trust you and I want you to stay away from Cady!" Chase said angrily. Someone started laughing, and it sounded like Brad.

"Man, you're just pissed that your girlfriend came running to me and not you." Brad said still laughing.

What is Brad talking about? I didn't go running to him for anything. Yeah he helped me remember Bani's number, but that was it.

"Whatever. I don't believe shit that comes out your mouth. There's something up with you that's wrong and Cady will see it too." Chase said.

"You're just jealous cuz she might want me and not you, dude. So you need to deal with it and move on." Brad said. "The way she kissed me, there's no way she was thinking about you." Brad said.

There was a loud noise and a grunt, "I'll kill you before I let you near her!" Chase yelled. I couldn't take it anymore.

I opened the door and ran in. Chase and Brad were on the floor fighting, "Stop it, now!" I yelled as I ran over and grabbed Chase's arm trying to pull him off of Brad. Chase stopped in mid swing and looked up at me. I could see the anger and hurt in his eyes. Chase had ahold of Brad's shirt, threw him down on the floor.

"What's wrong with you two!" I yelled as I grabbed Chase's arm and pulled him around to face me. "I can't believe you guys! Chase, what the hell is wrong with you?" I asked. "You could've killed him." I said angrily

"What's wrong with me? This prick talks shit on you and you're blaming me for it? That's messed up, Cady." Chase said as he turns toward the door to walk out.

"Chase wait, I'm not blaming you, I just want to know what's goin on." I said. "I heard some of the stuff you guys said, so trust me I'm not blaming you." I said as I spun around to look at Brad, "And what's this shit about us kissing?" I asked Brad.

"Umm…I didn't really say…" Brad started to say.

"Yes you did, I heard what you said. Now you need to tell the damn truth." I said interrupting Brad. I glanced at Chase. He had a smug smile on his face, "Don't look like you didn't do anything either." I said.

Chase looked down, "Sorry, but he shouldn't talk shit on you like that."

"No he shouldn't have, but I will take care of Brad, not you. Now, both of you get out, so I can fix this jeep, and clean up the mess you guys made." I said as I started pushing Chase out the door.

"But, I wanted to help you." Brad said looking hurt.

"You're not helping her do anything." Chase growled.

I threw my hands up in the air, "Both of you get out! I don't want to see either of you again! And if you don't leave now I'll shoot both of you in the ass with a lightning bolt!" I yelled. I could feel my eyes turn gold. Brad's eyes went wide, as he backed away towards the door.

Chase started to walk towards me, "Cady…" I shot a lightning bolt right next to his feet. He jumped back, with a look of shock on his face. I wanted to cry when I looked into his eyes and saw the hurt in them, but I was tired of all the fighting and yelling. I just wanted to be by myself.

"Please Chase, get out." I said quietly.

Chase hung his head down, walking near the door, "Sorry," he mumbled as he closed the door behind him.

I went to pick up the tools that were thrown all over due to the fight, "Men, suck." I mumbled to myself.

I worked for hours on the broken down jeep. If something could be wrong with it, it was. I always had loved working on cars. I focused all my thoughts on the car so I didn't have time to think of anything else. When there was nothing else I could do manually, I decided it was time to use some magic.

As I was working to make the jeep perfect again, I started thinking about this house that we were staying illegally. It's a great house with lots of room and I loved it, and I decided right then as soon as I got done with the jeep I was going to go into town and buy it.

After a few more hours, I was done. I went into the house to clean up a little before I going into town. I went up to my room to find a clean shirt. Unfortunately, I still had to wear one of Chases' shirts. That's another thing I have to do when I get into town. Buy some freaking clothes.

I was down the stairs when I saw Chase standing at the end of the staircase, "Hey, I was just goin to get a new shirt, but I saw you goin up, so I thought I would wait till you were done." Chase said quietly.

"I'm done. Oh I had to grab one of your shirts again. Sorry." I said.

Chase slightly smiled, "its ok, they still look better on you then me, any day."

I chuckled, "Thanks. I'm goin to town for some stuff we'll need here. Do you need anything?" I asked.

"No, I'm good. I guess you that jeep running then?" he asked.

"Yeah, I did most of the work myself, but then I got frustrated and used magic for the rest, but it looks good now." I said. It felt awkward talking to Chase, but I didn't want him to stop talking to me. We stood there not saying anything, so I decided it was time to go, "Well I guess I should get goin." I said.

Chase moved closer to me, and my back was up against the wall. He came inches from my face, and I thought he might kiss me, and I realized that I really wanted him to. Instead, he whispered, "I'm sorry about what happened out in the garage. And about what happened upstairs earlier. I just need to know what it is you want."

I stood there not saying anything, I just gazed into his bright green eyes. As I gazed, I saw my life and Chase's. We were sitting on a porch swing watching the sun go down. We were older, a lot older, and I could see kids playing out in the yards having fun…

"Well, I guess I got my answer." Chase said bringing me back to reality. He then turned and walked two steps at a time up the stairs. I wasn't sure what to do. I wish Bani would hurry up and get here. She would tell me what I needed to hear and tell what a dumbass I was being. I shook my head and went out the front door to go to town.

Twenty-two

It took about twenty minutes to get into town. I found a little shop where I bought a couple of new shirts and a few pairs of jeans as well as a load of under clothes. I called Bani to make sure they were on their way and to make sure the money my parents left me was now in the bank. When she said yes on both, I headed over to the bank to see who owned the mansion I wanted. I walked into the bank and up to a bank manager, "Hello, my name is Catalina Ashferd, and I need to speak with someone about the mansion at the edge of town?" I asked the bank manager.

"Oh yes, well that would be me, young lady." The bank manager said. "How may I help you?" he asked. He was a short bald man that needed to lose a few pounds.

"Well, I would like to know how I would…umm well I…I want to buy it." I said quietly.

He started laughing, "Oh honey, is this a prank? You can't possibly be serious? Do you know how much something like that would cost?" He asked.

I couldn't believe he thought I was kidding. "No, it's not a prank, and yes, I'm very much serious. I want to buy the mansion on the hill. Now you can either tell me how much it is or I'll take my business elsewhere." I said angrily

"Well, with the mansion and the acres, I would have to look it up, but I believe it's about one point two million dollars." The bank manager said.

I smiled, "Go make sure that's how much it is, and then draw up the paper work. I would like today, please."

The bank manager practically ran over to his computer and typed in some information. When he returned he had a big smile on his face, "Yes, Miss Ashferd, I was correct about the price. It's one point two million dollars, would you still like to have the property?"

I smiled, "Yes, I would." I pulled out the bank information that Bani had given me on the phone. I handed him the paper. "Here is my bank information. Can we have this done today?" I asked.

He looked down at the paper and went back to his computer. His eyes went wide as he came back over to where I was standing. "Miss Ashferd, everything will be ready within the hour, will that work for you?" he said, still wide eyed and smiling.

"Yes, that will be great, thank you. I would like the water and electricity on within that hour also." I said smiling.

"Oh yes, everything will be on and ready for you to move in today if you wish." He said trying not to jump up and down with joy over the sale he just made.

"Thank you, I'll be back in an hour to get the deed." I said as I walked out of the bank. I walked around the town for a bit. It was a small town. It had shops all the way down Main Street. Ballard also had one stop light at the end of town. I thought I could walk from one end to the other in twenty minutes.

As I walked down Main Street, I noticed different types of Supernatural's, but they were all young. I didn't see any older Supernatural's, just kids about thirteen or fourteen years of age. That's the most important time in a Supernatural's life.

I went into some more shops, but my mind kept going back to the night of the ritual. I looked down at my tattoo, remembering the night I got it, with my entire coven standing in the circle. I wish I could go back to that night, but would I have done anything different? Would I still have gone to the club? If I didn't, I wouldn't have found Chase, but Zane would still be alive and Vincent wouldn't be after me. Wow, I can really get myself into some messes.

I was also thinking about Chase. Would I give him up to change what happened that night? He gave up his pack for me, would I do the same? I knew I didn't want to lose him, but I didn't want to get hurt either. Oh, how my life sucks right now, I thought to myself.

After an hour of walking around, I headed back to the bank. As I walked in, the bank manager ran up to me. "Oh, Miss Ashferd, everything is ready for you to sign and as soon as you do, the property is yours." He said excitedly. I went with him to his office and sat down in the chair. He handed me the papers I needed to sign, as I started to read over them I noticed the acres.

"Umm there's a thousand acres included with the house?" I asked.

He looked up from the papers he was reading, "Yes, is there a problem? Is that not enough acreage?" he asked.

I shook my head, "No. no, I was just making sure. That's all." I said quickly.

We both signed everything we needed to, and as I stood up the bank manager took my hand in his and began shaking it, "It was a pleasure meeting you and doing business with you, Miss Ashferd."

"Thank you, it was a pleasure for me also." I said trying to sound older then I was. He walked me to the door and we said our goodbyes. I started the drive back to my new home. I also called Bani and told her everything would be ready for her when she got here. It would be a long two days till she's here.

I made it back to the house and walked in, and the twins and Nate were playing in the living room. I walked into the kitchen, and saw Avan, Violet, Brad and Cooper at the table. I sat down the bags down on the counter, "I bought some food for this place." I said as I went to the sink and made sure the water was on.

The water started coming out. "Oh my, how did you get the water to work?" Violet asked.

"Well while I was out shopping, I kinda bought this place." I said shrugging.

"Are you kidding? We don't have to hide every time someone comes around anymore?" Violet asked.

I laughed, "No, no more hiding and no more going out to get water. The electricity should be working, too."

Violet ran over to the light switch and turned it on. "Oh my heavens, it works!" she said as she ran over and hugged me. "Thank you so much Cady, but how could you afford this?" she whispered.

I hugged her back, "Don't worry about it, just know now you don't ever after to hide again." I stepped back from Violet.

"Umm, I have a friend and some of my other coven members coming, is there any way you guys can help me get this place ready for them?" I asked.

Violet smiled, "Of course, I'll help you." I looked over at Brad, Avan and Cooper, they all smiled.

"Well hell yeah, I'll help you do anything." Avan said.

Brad smiled, "I'll help too."

Cooper said, "Me too."

I beamed, "Thanks guys. Can you get the others to help too?" they shook their heads in agreement.

I left the kitchen to go find Chase. I didn't have to go far though, he was standing outside of the kitchen, "I thought I heard you come in," he said.

I started to smile until I saw his bag hanging over his shoulder. "Are you going somewhere?" I asked.

He hung his head down, "Yeah, I…I guess it's time for me to leave. I don't want to cause you anymore trouble," he said.

"What? Why, Chase?" I asked nervously.

Chase looked into my eyes, "Cady, I know what I want and that's you…but until you figure out what you want, I just don't think I'm helping you by being here."

I had tears in my eyes, "You said you would wait for me to figure it out! You said you would always be here with me no matter what!" I yelled.

I pushed him out of my way and ran up the stairs to my room, slamming it behind me. I sat down on my bed, burying my head in my hands. I heard the door open, but I didn't look up.

"Cady, I'm sorry. I thought this was what you would want." Chase said quietly. He sat down next to me, putting his arm around my shoulders. I felt the electricity flowing between us, and I knew that I didn't want him to leave. That much I knew for sure, but I didn't say anything. "Cady, tell me what you want me to do? If you want me to leave I will, if you want me to stay I will. I just don't know what you want me to do." He whispered in my hair.

"I don't want you to leave." I whispered.

He kissed the side of my head, "Then I won't. I really thought maybe it would be easier on you. I'm so sorry, Cady"

I looked into his eyes. Chase brought up his hand, taking his thumb rubbing the tear off my face, "I don't ever want to hurt you, I love you, Cady." I didn't say anything, I bent over bringing my lips to his, opening my mouth to let his tongue intertwine with mine. Finally, when we let go of each other, we were both breathless.

"We should really get this place cleaned up before Bani gets here," I said as I started to stand up.

Chase grabbed me by the waist, pulling me back down on him. I was now sitting on his lap, "Let's stay right here, just like this for a little longer." He said as he kissed my neck.

"We need to get this place cleaned up and get furniture in here." I said trying to get up again, but he wouldn't let go.

He looked up, "Why do we need furniture here? We'll be leaving soon…won't we?" he asked.

I slightly smiled, "Well, I kinda bought this place." Chase looked at me puzzled, I forgot I never got the chance to tell him what all happened. So, I told him about Brad coming in and helping me with a memory spell so I could call Bani. I went on to tell him that they were now coming here and the only way was to just buy the place. I also told him about how I got the money and how my Aunt Mable gave it to me on my eighteenth birthday.

When I was finally finished and had said everything I needed to, he kissed my neck again. "You've been through some shit. I'm so sorry, babe."

I kissed his lips and asked, "It's ok, now can we now get started?"

Chase gave a low growl, "Fine, but I'd rather stay here kissing you."

"Don't you growl at me, wolfboy. Now come on." I said chuckling, pulling him up with me.

Twenty-three

We all worked the next two days, cleaning and ordering furniture for every room. By the end of the second day we were finally done with everything. The house had beds, dressers and a desk in every bedroom. Every other room was filled will furniture, and the place looked great. Chase, Nate and the twins were in the game room playing pool, while Avan, Cooper and Violet were in the kitchen cooking dinner. Brad was out in the garage building something, but he wouldn't let anyone go in and see.

I was leaning against the game room door, watching Chase shoot his ball into the corner pocket. He looked up at me and smiled, "You wanna play partners, babe?" he asked me.

I started walking towards the pool table, but heard the doorbell. "Nope, I gotta get the door." I said as I turned around and headed to the front door.

I opened the door and Oma stood there looking at me with a wide smile, "Catalina! Oh, my heavens, are you ok?"

I smiled, "Hi Oma. I'm ok."

She came out and gave me a tight hug. "I'm so happy to see you, my child."

I hugged her back tightly, "Oh, Oma, I'm so glad you're ok. I was so worried. Are you sure you're ok? Where is Bani? Is everyone else in the coven ok?"

She giggled, "Slow down Catalina, I can't keep up with all your questions. You know I'm an old lady. Now let's go inside and talk." She looked behind me and saw everyone behind me. She smiled, "And who are your friends, Catalina."

I smiled, "I'm sorry Oma, this is Nate, Avan, Cooper, Violet and the twins Brit and Kate." I took ahold of Chase's hand, "And this is Chase. They've helped me out a lot, lately."

She looked down at our hands and then back up to the others. "Well, it's nice to meet you kids. Thank you for taking care of my Catalina, I am surprised she let you help her, though," she said, snickering.

They all said in unison, "Nice to meet you."

Oma hugged me again, "Oh child, we are going to have a long nice talk," She said as she glanced at Chase and smiled.

We all headed into the living room and Chase grabbed my hand, leaned down and whispered, "Catalina?"

I looked over at him, "Don't you dare, wolfboy" I whispered back.

He laughed quietly, "I like it." He said in low sexy voice. Great, I thought.

Chase took Oma's bag upstairs to her room, and Avan, Cooper and Violet went back into the kitchen. Nate took the twins back to the game room. I sat down next to

Oma. "Catalina, let's talk so you can tell me what's been going on."

Oma and I sat on her bed she told me how her and Bani had gone to work the day after I talked to them. Vincent had been standing by the door. As they walked up to him, he told them that I killed Eddie, and asked where I was. If they didn't tell him, he said he would kill everyone in the coven. They both told him they had no idea where I was. He got mad and threw a bunch of fireballs into the store. They went to run into the store, but when they got there, lava was running out the door. They ran to gather the other members of the coven and went to the safe house. They had stayed there until it was time to come to Ballard.

"That's awful Oma," I said.

"Yes, it was, now tell me what happened with you," Oma said.

I told her everything that had happened to me over the last four days. I told her everything about what happen at the club with Zane and Eddie. To Chase picking me over his pack and saying I was his mate, and how I found this place with the five kids in here. How they didn't know their main power and no one taught them any type of magic. They had to learn on their own. Finally, saying that Garrett said I was a Valkyrie and he knew my mother and she was one also. After I got it all out I said, "That's about all of it."

Oma took my hand and smiled, "Oh Catalina, you have been through everything from horrible to the best news. I'm sorry about what happen to Zane, but I'm also happy, for you, with Chase. From what you've told me, he sounds like a dream come true."

I squeezed her hand and smiled, "I think he is, but I'm also scared. What if he's not? Oma, I don't want to get hurt and I keep thinking that if I didn't go to the club that night… Zane would still be here."

Oma had a sad look, "Cady, I've always told you that everything happens for a reason. It can be good or bad, but it's what is destined. I do believe you and Zane were supposed to be there that night and even if you tried to change it, and not go. The end would've been the same, no matter what. I also believe that you finding Chase was no accident, you are destined to be together. He already knows this. The question now is…do you know this or even want this?"

I sat there thinking about what Oma just said. I knew that everything happened for a reason, I've always believed that. So, Zane and I going to that club was, what we were meant to do. If I had to pick between Chase or my coven…..I realized then I would pick Chase. There was no doubt in my mind.

I frowned, "Well crap, Oma." I put my head in my hands, asking, "What if I'm not cut out to be his mate? You know I'm not good with guys, in fact I suck at it."

Oma chuckled, "Catalina, you will do fine. It will come naturally for you. It already does for with him." I looked at her puzzled. She laughed, "Oh my child, I see the way he looks at you. It's nothing but pure love in his eyes when it comes to you. You just have to learn to let go and relax."

I slightly smiled, "That's easier said than done, but I'll try."

"That's all we can ever ask for. Now, to this Garrett man and what he said about you being a Valkyrie. He actually might be on to something," Oma said. I looked wide eyed at her. She held up her hand, "Let me explain, Catalina. The night of the ritual, I told you I would try and find something out about your tattoo and the lightning. I read many books looking up tattoos and lightning, and what it all meant. A lot of them pointed to the Valkyrie history. I'm not sure, but that may explain why your mother didn't want you around werewolves." Oma said explaining. I just sat there trying to take everything in. "Some Valkyries are known as *Göndul*, which means, magic wand or she-werewolf. I also found where they were shape shifters," Oma said.

I asked, "What does that exactly mean?"

"I'm not sure, Catalina. Maybe your mother thought if you were around wolves, you would shape shift into one. Honey, this was all that I read and could come up with. It doesn't mean anything though. I'm just throwing out ideas, I really do not want to worry you. I do think after this ordeal is over with Vincent... you should start trying to find your parents again. They're the only ones that can tell you everything you need to know," Oma said.

"Oma, I don't even know where to start looking for them, but your right I do need to know the truth. I had a dream that I was standing next to Chase one minute and then the next I was a wolf. I was hoping it was just a dream. But after all the shi...stuff is over, I'll start looking again for my parents. I need to know what's going on." I said.

Oma stood up and as followed, she gave me a hug and said, "Your dreams tell you a lot, child. Now you need to get some rest and we will start planning what to do about Vincent in the morning."

I frowned, "You're the one that needs rest Oma, you're the one that had a long drive." I said smiling, "and thank you Oma, thank you for everything." She hugged me again and we walked out of the room to the main hall, where the front door was.

Everyone from the coven was standing there in the foyer, they must've gathered there while I was talking to Oma.

It didn't take me long to find Chase. He was leaning against the wall with his arms folded, staring at the door, I had just come out of. I smiled, and in a few steps he was right next to me, asking, "Did everything go, ok? Are you ok?"

"Yes I'm fine, we had a good talk. I just have so much in my head. I don't know how to put it all together, if that makes any sense at all." I said.

Chase put his arm around my shoulders and said with a caring tone, "It makes perfect sense, babe. We can talk about it and you can get it all out. I'm right here if you need me."

I took his hand, "Thanks, I would love that."

He beamed showing his dimples and perfect white straight teeth. He leaned down and whispered in my ear, "Can I kiss you now?" I turned red and he started laughing, so I smacked him upside the head. He pulled me close to him and kissed the top of my head, "Just trying to make you feel better." I relaxed against his chest thinking about everything Oma had said. He does make me feel better, I thought to myself.

"Move, I said move!" someone yelled from the back of the room. Just then everyone started moving out of

Bani's way, as she came rushing through. I went running to meet you half way, she crashed into me, hugging me and crying, "Oh my heavens, Cady! I'm sorry about what happen to Zane, are you ok? Are you hurt? Why the hell didn't you call me sooner?" she looked behind me, "Who's the three hot wolves behind you?" she asked. She was talking so fast I just hugged her tighter.

"It's a long story, but I'll fill you in on all of it. I'm sorry about Zane, too, Bani, I couldn't save him," I cried.

She pulled back from our embrace and looked at me, "Cady, it wasn't your fault, so quit blaming yourself." I knew she would know what I was feeling.

I smiled slightly, "Thanks Bani, I'm just so glad you're here." She waved it off like it was no big deal.

She looked at me and smiled, "Now the most important question. Are you ok?"

I said, "Yeah I'm fine."

She beamed, "Good, I was worried like hell. Now, next important question, who the hell are the three hot wolves back there?"

I laughed, "Well, let me introduce you to them."

She leaned in and whispered, "Ok, that guy has it bad for you, my friend"

I looked at her puzzled, "What? Why would you say that?"

She giggled, "Ok, the hot one with the blond hair and green eyes can't take his eyes off of you. He looks at you with pure love in those amazing eyes. That's why I said that."

I started pulling her towards the guys. We stopped in front of them and we both smiled. Chase looked over at me and smiled. "Bani, this is Avan, Nate, Cooper, Violet, Brad and the twins Brit and Kate and this is Chase. Guys, this is my best friend, Bani," I said smiling.

Nate stepped up and smiled, "Nice to meet you, Bani."

Bani grinned ear to ear, "Well, nice to meet you too Nate." Nate took Bani's hand in his and kissed it.

Chase came to stand by me leaning to whisper in my ear, "How are you holding up, you doing ok?" I smiled and shook my head yes.

Everyone was coming up to me hugging me saying how glad they were that I was safe and saying how sorry they were about Zane.

Aunt Mable walked up to me with a sour look on her face, "Cady, I see that you are fine. I also see that not only did you get yourself in trouble again, but this time you've put the whole coven at risk." She was such a bitch.

I started to say, "Aunt....."

Chase interrupted me, "Cady, didn't do anything wrong." He growled.

Aunt Mable gave him a dry look then looked the same way back at me.

"Oh yes, let's not forget you brought wolves in here also. Your mother would be furious you if she knew you were with a wolf." She said fuming.

She was pissing me off, "Don't talk about my mother!"

"That's enough Mable, if you don't stop right now, you may leave!" Oma roared.

Mable's eyes went wide in horror. "But Oma…"

Oma raised your hand, "Your choice Mable, you are the one that wanted to come here, so stop the nonsense or leave."

Mable walked away muttering to herself, "Fine, but when all hell breaks loose. Don't say I didn't warn everyone."

Bani smiled, "She's such a bitch, are you ok?"

I rolled my eyes, "I wish everybody would quit asking me that, I'm fine."

She hit me on the shoulder, "That's for not calling me for days! You know how much I worry!" she said trying to sound mad.

I wrinkled my brows saying, "You ass, quit hitting me. I would have called you sooner, but as you know, I kinda lost my phone and all my numbers. Wolfboy, here didn't grab it." I said pointing my thumb at Chase.

He just shrugged, "I've never needed one, so I didn't think about grabbing it."

Bani rolled her eyes and laughed which made me laugh with her. She pulled me over to a corner where we were alone, and said, "Spill it." I told her the whole story I told Oma. When I got to the part about Zane we cried, then when I told her about the mating thing with Chase she threw her hands up to her mouth, "Oh my heavens! I'm sooo happy for you!"

"Shhh, not so loud, Bani!" I whispered loudly.

She begin whispering, "Oh sorry, I can't believe it. You go and blow off every guy in and out of town. I didn't think you would ever pick someone. You were just waiting for some Greek god to sweep you off your feet. Damn girl, when you do find one, you find a good one. So how's he in bed? Tell me everything!"

I started laughing, "Yeah, I guess he did sweep me off my feet, literally. I was passed out when he took me to his house, and for the whole bed thing." I shrugged, "I don't know about that, we haven't….we haven't done anything."

Bani's eyes went wide, "Are you freakin kidding me, Cady! Why the hell not?"

I took a deep breath and said, " I don't know. I was scared, but now I'm ok. I know what and who I want." I smiled, "I want him."

Bani smiled glancing over at Chase, then back at me, "I have a feeling he won't hurt you. In fact, the way he looks at you, I can guarantee it. I've never seen a guy look so in love before. So, you better be jumping on him tonight or I'll be kicking your ass tomorrow!"

I smacked her on the shoulder laughing, "That will be the day, when you can kick my ass." We both started laughing again heading back to where the guys were. As soon as we got close, Chase looked up and over at me. We both smiled as our eyes met I strolled over to him and took his hand. He brought my hand up to his lips kissing my palm.

We all were standing there talking, and Bani was telling some old story from our past. Nate couldn't take his eyes off of her. Chase, Violet and Avan were also listening and laughing, when she came to a funny part in her story. I just shook my head over how embarrassing it all was.

"Ok, everyone, it's been a long day and I just want to say goodnight. I'll see you all in the morning," Oma said. She got up and went to her room. Chase helped Oma up the stairs and to her room. The rest of us started showing everyone else to their rooms. We all said goodnight and headed to our rooms.

Chase and I went up to our room, it now had a nice king size bed with two dressers, one for each of us and a desk in the corner. "Do you want to wear one of my shirts?" Chase asked

I shook my head, "No that's ok, I bought some pj's at the store the other day." I went over to look through my dresser, finding a pair of shorts and tank top, both silk.

I looked at Chase he smiled, "I like seeing you in my shirts." I raised my brow to him, he smiled even more, "Ok, I'll turn around."

He turned and I threw my clothes on fast. I said, "Ok, I'm done."

He turned back around looked at me raising his brows doing a circulator motion with his finger, "Your turn." I laughed turning around. "Ok, I'm ready now," Chase said. I turned around and found him in nothing but his boxer shorts. It's now or never, I thought. I gazed into eyes and smiled.

I strolled over to him and wrapped my arms around his neck, stood up on my toes and started kissing him passionately. Chase grabbed me around the waist, lifting me up closer to him. I wrapped my legs around his waist. His kiss was full of passion and hunger, and when his tongue came out, it met mine. They started intertwining with each other. Chase carried me over to the bed and placed me down gently, with him on top of me. I pulled his hair to bring him closer to me, kissing him harder. He pulled his head slightly back, breathing hard and looking into the eyes. His eyes were shining bright green, and full of desire, "I think I need to go take a cold shower." He smiled, as he started to get up.

I smiled, "Not tonight." I pulled him back to me and started kissing him again, and he didn't refuse. He crushed his mouth on mine. I could feel the electricity flowing between us. I moved my hands down his back to his shorts.

He moved his lips to my chin, down my neck, over to my ear and whispered, "Are you sure this is what you want? You know what this means to me."

I moved my hands back up to each side of his face. I turned him to face me looked him straight in the eyes and whispered, "I've never been more sure than I am right now. I know what I want. I want you, Chase, now and forever."

He brought his lips down to mine with more passion then I ever felt before. His hand moved down my side stopping at the hem of my tank top. His hand was trembling as he slid it under my top, touching my bare skin. I trembled with delight as his hand came up caressing my boobs. Chase pulled his lips back slightly, "If you want me to stop I will…. I'll never do anything you don't want me to do." He said, brushing his lips against mine. His eyes were glowing bright green. I didn't say anything. I just put my hands on his back and pulled him closer to me, and that night made love to the man of my dreams.

Twenty-four

We stayed side by side for some time, neither one of us talking. He was stroking my hair, while I was thinking about what we had just done. Bani always said when she slept with a guy it lasted maybe, fifteen minutes. I'm not sure what kind of guys she slept with, but they need to take lessons from Chase. That was way longer than any fifteen minutes. I would say closer to forty-five minutes.

He kissed the top of my head, "Now that you have seduced me and bitten me, do you want to talk about what happened tonight?"

I looked up at him smacking him in the chest smiling, "I did not seduce you, and biting was just a perk, for me."

He laughed, "I'm kidding, and you can seduce or bite me anytime you want."

"Your such an…." He stopped me from talking by kissing me.

He pulled back after the kiss and asked, "Do want to talk about what happened tonight?"

I looked at him like I was confused, "I figured you knew what just happened here tonight?"

He squeezed me tighter, "Oh babe, I know what just happened here and loved every minute of it. Even ready to do it all over again right now, but I was talking about your talk with Oma."

I chuckled, "I know what you were talking about. Well, she told me that I might be a Valkyrie, but she's not sure. Since my parents disappeared there's no way to find out I guess."

"What exactly happened with your parents? I know you've been looking for them, but why?" he asked.

I sat there for a minute thinking, "There's not really too much to say," I shrugged.

"I woke up the day after my thirteenth birthday and they were nowhere to be found. I looked everywhere for them. That night, Aunt Mable showed up and said she was there to take care of me until my parents decided to come back. They never did and no one has heard from them since." I said.

He kissed lightly on the lips, "I'm sorry, babe that had to be so hard."

I laughed, "It was harder living with my Aunt. She was horrible and mean. I couldn't do anything right or fast enough for her. So, the day I turned eighteen she moved out and didn't look back."

"Yeah, she doesn't seem to be very nice." Chase said. "You know, we could start looking for them. After this shit with Vincent, is solved." Chase said.

"You would help me, look for them?" I asked quietly.

Chase brought his hand to my face, stroking my jaw line. "Catalina, I would do anything for you. I don't know how many times I need to tell you." He brought my face up to look at him, "But I'll tell you every day or even every hour, until you start believing me." He kissed my lips lightly, brushing his back and forth with mine, "Face it babe, you're stuck with me," he whispered.

"I can live with that," I whispered back, and then I raised my brow. "Hey, what's the deal with calling me, Catalina? Everyone calls me, Cady."

He looked at me and smiled, "I told you, I like Catalina. Besides, I'm not everyone. I'm the one who will be spending the rest my life, with you." I just smiled reaching up and kissed him again. We finally fell asleep in each other's arms.

"Catalina, are you going to sleep all day? Or am I gonna have to figure out a way to wake you up?" Chase asked as he started kissing down my neck to my collar bone.

I chuckled between kisses, "Well, good morning to you."

"If I can wake up to you, like this every morning... I'll never leave the bed. Your beautiful, Catalina." Chase said as he continued kissing me. We finally got out of bed, after making love again.

I headed to the bathroom to take a shower, with Chase right behind me, "Don't think about it, wolfboy." I said smiling.

Chase gave a sad puppy eye look, "What, you really won't let me take a shower with you?"

"No, there's like twenty people here. I'm just hopin' no one heard us. Now I have to get in and out fast to help start breakfast." I said as I started shutting the door.

He grabbed the door, "I can so be in and out fast."

I wrinkled my brows, "you, in and out fast? I don't think you can, wolfboy. Now, move so I can get done, then you can take one."

"Ok, I guess, I'll go start breakfast then." Chase said as he gave me a quick kiss and headed to the kitchen.

There wasn't much done that week, we all tried to figure out what Vincent had in mind. We decided that I should stay here, while the coven went back to their houses. Of course, Bani said she was going the same place I was going. She wouldn't let me out of her sight again. I just laughed, I think it had more to do with Nate then me.

I would see them glancing over at each other and smile. I hope they do end up together, that would good, I thought.

Avan finally loosened up around me, so we all seemed to be getting along well. The guys would go out some nights to change in their wolf form, while Bani and I would practice our magic and show Violet, Cooper and

Brad how to tap into theirs. Oma worked with the twins and their magic. Brad kept disappearing out in the garage for hours at a time.

"I can't believe we've been here for two weeks." I said as I lay next to Chase in bed one night.

"Me neither, but I kinda can't wait till everyone leaves. I want to have you all to myself, well, and have you in every room here." Chase said in a low sexy growl, as he kissed my neck.

"You are such a perv. You do realize that, right." I said laughing.

"Yup, I sure do, babe." He said laughing.

"How would you feel about us living here, instead of going back to Belton or the Ozarks?" I asked quietly.

Chase looked at me and smiled. "I'll go wherever you want us to go, and besides I kinda like here too." He then continued to kiss my neck.

There was a bang on the door and we both jumped, we stopped what we were doing and looked over at the door.

"Everyone get up now! Emergency meeting!!" someone yelled through the door.

Chase looked down at me and kissed my neck, "I can't believe this," He growled. I couldn't believe it either what on earth could be going on.

We both got out of bed and got dressed we were heading to the door when grabbed my arm and pulled me around facing him. His eyes still shinning bright, he bent down kissing my lips, cheek, and neck up to my ear. In a low sexy as hell growl he said, "We'll continue this and other things, later."

I kissed his neck whispering, "hell yeah, we will." He brought his lips back to mine pushing me back into the wall. We could hear running feet on the other side.

Chase hung his head down, "We better go see what's going on."

I chuckled, "good idea, or I'm gonna forget about them and go for round two with you."

"Can we just do that?" Chase asked with his puppy eyes and happy grin.

I laughed, "No, it could be something important." We walked out into the hallway heading towards the common area where everyone could meet. Oma was standing there talking to one of the coven members intensely. We made our way over to where she was, "Oma, what's going on?" I asked.

Oma took my hand, "Oh Catalina, Zane's mother just called, and….and he took Tamra."

My eyes went wide in shock, I felt dizzy almost falling back. Chase grabbed my arm to steady me. "Who…who took her Oma!" I said almost yelling.

Twenty-Five

"Vincent took her and it's all your fault. You should have never killed Eddie. Vincent knows you're here, now." Aunt Mable said behind me.

I whipped around and glared at her, "How'd he know I was here? No one knew I was here until I told the coven!" I said accusing. I could feel the tingling in my eyes.

Aunt Mable stepped back away from me, and Chase moved to stand in front of me blocking me from Aunt Mable. Putting his hands on my shoulders, "Cady, you need to calm down. You need to take some deep breaths and calm down." He said in a soothing voice. I closed my eyes, taking in a deep breath, trying to settle down so my eyes would change back.

"She's evil!! Did you see her eyes change to gold! That's not natural that's evil and she brought it to us!" Aunt Mable shouted while pointing at me.

"Mable, that's enough!" Oma shouted back. Oma came and stood in front of me facing everyone else, "Our Catalina, is not by any means evil. She is and as always been different, powerful yes, but evil never." She hissed. "We all have known this from the time she was thirteen. For heaven sakes Mable, you took care of her for five years. How could you say such a thing!" she said pointing her finger at Aunt Mable.

"I'm speaking the truth! That's why her parents left her!" Aunt Mable shouted.

"You need to leave and leave now!" Oma shouted. Aunt Mable stormed off towards her room slamming her door behind her.

Oma turned and looked at me with sad eyes, "Catalina, forget what she said, she's crazy. What we need to do now is figure out why he took Tamra."

I had tears in my eyes, "Ok, Oma. Why would he take Tamra, she's only sixteen? She's a good kid, his son already took Zane from us why would his dad take her?" I asked.

Tamra was Zane's little sister, she would come and hang out with us sometimes. She thought it made her cooler, but she was already cool. He must've taken her because of me. To get back at me for Eddie, but he had taken Zane from me already. Why take someone else from me too?

"Cady, we'll figure it out and find her, but you've been through a lot lately. Maybe you should go lie down and rest for a while?" Chase said taking a hold of my hand.

"I agree with Chase, Catalina, you need to rest. It's the middle of the night and in the morning we'll try and figure this out. If I come up with something tonight, I'll come and get you." Oma said.

"I don't need to rest, I need to get out of here for a while." I said.

"Cady, that's not a good idea. We don't know what or who is out there." Bani said.

"I'll be fine, I just need to run for a while and think," I shrugged. "It might help me think of something to do to get Tamra back. I won't go far and I'll stay in the woods, besides, no one knows where this house is. So it'll be fine." I said

"Cady, can I talk to you for a minute please?" Chase asked. We walked back into our room I was digging through my dresser for a pair of sweat pants and shirt. Chase stood by the door arms crossed over his chest looking down. Finally he looked up at me, "Are we even going to talk about this?"

"There's nothing to talk about Chase, I just want…I need to exercise to get out all the shit that's been building up inside me." I said.

Chase shook his head and started walking to his dresser, "Ok, I get what you're saying, I do. So I'll go running with you. You can think and I can make sure your safe, ok?"

"No Chase, it's not ok, I run by myself so I can think." I said.

"Please don't push me away and try and do everything yourself." Chase said.

"I'm pushing you away, that's not what I'm doing. I'm just trying to figure this out in my head and when I do, I'll come back. We can talk about it then and try to figure out what to do to get Tamra back." I said.

I walked up to him putting my hands on his chest. He reached his hands down to hold my face, kissing me lightly on my lips, then put his forehead on mine and whispered, "I don't want to lose you, I just found you. I love you, Catalina."

I grabbed his shirt tight in my fist pulling him down to my lips kissing him hard. I pulled back my head slightly, "I love you too, wolfboy."

His eyes shinned as he kissed me again lightly, "Please be careful and come back to me soon."

I smiled, "I will and thank you for understanding. I'll be back in an hour, tops."

He smiled back, "You better be or I'll get all wolfish on your ass."

I raised my brow, "Oh I…"

He kissed me and I couldn't finish what I was saying. He pulled back still brushing my lips with his, "Just be careful, that's all I'm asking."

I got dressed in my sweats and headed out the door. Bani stopped me, "This isn't your fault, Cady. No matter what that bitch says. We all know and love you."

I smiled, "Thanks, Bani." I walked outside and started stretching my legs and arms. I was jogging, thinking about everything that had happened, trying to figure out how to get Tamra back.

She must be so scared right now and I would do anything to get her back. Not just for her, but for Zane. I miss him so much; he always knew how to make me feel better. Hell, he would tell me what to do.

All of a sudden something hit me in the back of the head and I went down on my knees. I shook my head trying to get my vision back. I looked over my shoulder to see who hit me. A man smiled and hit me with something again suddenly everything went black....

I stood in nothing but blackness. As I stood there, everything started getting hazy, and flashes of light came and went. It's like I was watching a movie screen out of focus. I was only getting glimpse, of several different things. I saw the same pink and black flowers as in my first dream.

There I stood in the middle of a field with flowers all around me, and I was kissing my dream guy. He lifted his head up slightly, and I could see his bright green eyes. I looked closer trying to see his face, he hugged me and for the first time I saw his face....it was Chase! I can't believe all this time my dream guy was Chase. I could see the lava coming down the hill. Why weren't we running or something? I can't believe I would just stand there. Then the light switched, "Damn, I wanted to see what happens next." I quietly said to myself.

The light went out and then back on. This time I saw Chase and myself in another field. He had just turned into his wolf form, and he had his same bright green eyes. His fur was golden ash blond, and he was absolutely beautiful. I changed into a wolf, and my eyes were the same. My fur was blond with a hint of red in it! "What the hell" I muttered to myself.

My dream switched again and there was Aunt Mable and Vincent kissing each other. Well, that's just gross.

The light switched again, and this time I saw Tamra tied up in a chair. Three men took turns hitting her with something. I looked closer and saw Zane on the other side of her, tied to a pole.

Zane lifted his head up and showed his fangs, it looked like he was hissing at Tamra. Oh, man, he's a vampire! Those sons of bitches turned him into a blood sucking machine! He looked like he was trying to fight them off to get to her, but he wasn't using his power. Why isn't he using his ice power to break the ropes? Why isn't Tamra using her fire? I don't get it. Someone walked in, I started trying to focus on who it was. It was two people a man and woman, is that? Is that? Crap, it changed again.

This time it looks like a forest of some kind with women dressed in short skirts and tops made of animal skin. They are all running towards something I can't see, but they looked pissed. One looked over her shoulder and I could see her eyes. They were pure gold! "Well this is just freaking crazy! What the hell is going on here?" *I yelled at the screen.*

This time when it changed I saw Chase again. He was running through the woods yelling something Bani, Nate and Avan were with him. They all were looking for something.

Chase ran up to something on the ground and he bent down to smell it, and yelled, "Cady!"

He started running through the woods. Oh, my heavens I heard him.

I yelled, "Chase!" *He stopped in his tracks looking around. He must've heard me,* "Chase, can you hear me?"

He was looking everywhere, "Cady, I can hear you! Where are you?"

"I don't know where I am, I think I'm dreaming though." I shouted.

He looked confused, "Dreaming? If you were dreaming then how the hell do I hear you? Babe, I'm awake and looking for you. You've been gone for hours. Please tell me where you are?" he begged.

"I don't know where I'm at, all I remember is running in the woods and....and someone hit me! Maybe they knocked me out, but...but I don't know how you can hear me," I said.

Bani, Nate and Avan were all looking at Chase like he had completely lost his mind. Bani said something I couldn't hear. "I can hear, Cady," Chase said to Bani. "Babe, I don't know how we can hear each other. They can't hear you, but I don't care why or how, I'm just so glad I can. I'll find you, I promise," Chase said.

"How? I don't even know where I'm at." I cried.

"Ba...don't....I...fi..." Chase was trying to say something, but it kept going in and out.

"Chase, I can't understand you! What did you say?" Chase started looking around again throwing his hands in the air.

"Ca...I...can't...y...what...d....you...s..?" Chase tried to say.

The screen started flickering on and off. "No, Chase!" I screamed.

Chase yelled back, "Catalina!"

I'm losing the picture, but why? It flickered more, and then I felt a sharp pain on my face, "Ouch, son of a bit..."

Everything went black.....

Twenty-Six

"Wake up honey," someone said. I shook my head, it was pounding so hard, I thought it was going to kill me. I went to touch my cheek, but couldn't move my hand. I tried to open my eyes, but it hurt so bad. "I said, wake the hell up!" that same someone said. I felt him smack me again.

"Will you quit, freaking hitting me?" I said getting pissed.

"Then you need to look at me, honey." He said. Why does he keep calling me honey? Do I look like a damn honey bee? I made my eyes open but everything was blurry. I tried focusing and finally I could see. I looked up to see who smacked me. My eyes went wide! It couldn't be! Oh, my heavens, no it couldn't freaking be!

"Vincent?" I asked in barely a whisper.

He smiled, "Nice to see you again, honey."

"Vincent, please let me explain, what happen with Eddie? Tamra had nothing to do with any of this." I said fearfully.

Vincent just smiled, "You can tell me all about how you killed my one and only son. It really doesn't matter to me what you say. You, Tamra and your other friends, are all dead anyway. The only thing I care about is how I'm going to make you suffer, before I kill you. I can't have your kind running around, now can I." he said as he walked to a door. What the hell is he talking about, my *kind* is everywhere.

I tried to freeze the ropes, but nothing happen. Vincent turned and laughed, "Oh yes, I forgot to tell you the best part. When you were knocked out, my boys gave you a serum to block all your witch powers." Then he went out the door laughing.

I looked around to see if I could figure out where the hell I was. The room itself was dark and hard to see.

"Cady, is that you? Please tell me it's you?" Well, who the hell was that? I looked around to see if I could find out who was talking. In the corner sat another chair with someone on it. I waited till my eyes focused on the person. It looked like a girl with long hair, maybe Tamra, but I couldn't be sure.

So I asked, "Umm Tamra, is that you?"

"Oh Cady, it is you! Yeah it's me, it's Tamra! I'm so glad to see you, well I wish it was somewhere else, but you know what I mean!" she said, talking really fast.

"Tamra, do you know where we are?" I asked hoping.

She sat there for a while before she finally answered, "I...I don't know, but I think it's in a basement of some kind. I do know we're still in Belton through. Does that help any?"

"Yeah, that helps a lot Tamra." I said "We need...." I stopped talking, when someone came into the room.

"Oh please, don't stop talking on my account. I'll just entertain myself, until you two are done." A voice said as he walked into the room. As he got closer, I could start to make out his face. He had red hair and black eyes, he looked to be about 6'2 and skinny as a pole.

"Who are you?" I asked feeling snippy. He just laughed, walking up and getting inches from my face. I was staring in the eyes of a vampire, not just any vampire. The vampire that killed Zane!

"You don't remember me, sweetheart?" he said smiling.

I started struggling with the rope on my hands, "I'm going to kill you, you stupid son of a bitch!" I yelled, trying to get free.

He just chuckled, "Aww, yes you do remember me." He reached up grabbing my hair, yanking it back, and exposing my neck, "I wonder how you taste?" I tried to move my head, but his grip was too tight. My hands were tied and he had my head. All I could think was, this blood sucking asshole was going to drain me, like he did Zane

I moved my foot and realized they weren't tied to anything. I smiled, "You want to know how good I taste? Well taste this, you ass!" I said as I brought my knee up to between his legs hard, and he went to his knees. Then I kicked him as hard as I could in the gut. He went flying across the room, hitting the wall.

He shook his head a few times and in a blink of an eye he was back in my face, snarling, "I'm going to make you pay for that, you little bitch!"

He punched me in the face then my stomach. I grunted, but never said a word. I wasn't about to give this ass any satisfaction. I could kick him again, but he'll just come back and hit me harder. I don't want that to happen, I need my strength for when I get out of here.

He hit me again, "I'm going to love to kill you, but first we'll have some fun." He reached up and grabbed my shirt, tearing it off of me.

"Leave her alone! Leave her alone!" Tamra kept yelling. He acted like he didn't even hear her.

Then he brought his face up to my neck, kissing and licking it, "Aww yes sweetheart, we are going to have a lot of fun together." He continued to kiss and lick down my neck.

Tamra kept yelling as loud as she could and crying. I wanted to puke my guts up, with just the thought of him touching me.

His other hand was sliding down to the edge of my sweat pants, he stopped at the hem. He looked up at me, but didn't say anything, just smiled. He started moving his hand into my sweats.

I need to get out of this now! It's starting to look like a very scary movie, just waiting to happen. I looked down at him, "Hey, I don't even know your name. That's really not fair is it? I mean with you groping me and all," I said in my sweetest voice.

He looked at me with a confused look, "You want to know my name, sweetheart? Cause I'll be doing more than just groping you, as you put it," he said harshly. I don't care how he says it, I just need him to keep him talking and keep his hands off of me.

"I got that part, but what name will I yell out when…when I get excited?" I asked bashfully.

He laughed loudly at that. He put his hand on my face and with a sweet tone he said, "You can yell out all you want, but if you need a name to scream, then it's Ian."

Just then someone else came through the door. Oh, great, it's freaking Vincent. As he walked in he asked, "Ian, I hope you're not doing anything nasty to our guest?" Great. I hope they're here for him and not me.

"No, just entertaining her, that's all," Ian said.

Entertaining me his ass! I want nothing more than to kick the living shit out of this asshole.

"Well, I brought someone else to entertain her," Vincent said smiling over at me. Someone else brought in a man with his head down, barely standing on his feet. He took him over to a pole in the middle of the room, and tied him up.

"Now, you all get reacquainted again, and I'll see you soon. You have a good day, Cady. Come along Ian, we need to go and get ready." Vincent said as he was leaving.

Ian looked over at me and smiled, "I'll see you soon, Cady. We can finish what we started."

I just stared him down. If that prick wasn't already on the top of my list to kill, he sure the hell would be now. Before he left, he rammed his fist into my head, and again everything went black....

Twenty-Seven

I was standing in the living room of my house, and there was a lot yelling going on. I went to where the yelling was coming from. There, in the ball room, were Bani, Nate, Avan, Oma and Chase, and they were all yelling at each other.

Chase was yelling, "I'm going after her!"

Oma was shaking her head, "Chase, you don't know where she is. We need to come up with a plan."

"My only plan is to go find her and make sure she's safe." Chase growled.

Bani held up her hand. "I get it, I do. I want nothing more than to go and find her, but Oma is right. We have no clue as to where she's at." Ok, I need to do something, because Chase is gonna go crazy if he doesn't get out of there .

Chase threw up his hands, "I will go myself if I....."

I walked up behind him and said, "Chase, can you hear me?"

He stopped in mid-sentence, looking around. He quietly said, "Yes."

"Ok, good, now go into our room so I can talk to you," I said. He started walking out of the room.

Bani looked over at him, "Chase, where are you going?"

"I need a minute to myself, ok?" Chase said quickly as he left the room. I followed him into the bedroom. He looked around, "Cady, are you here, babe?" I stared at him. He looked so sad and worried.

"I'm here Chase, but I don't know how long I'll be asleep." I said. I didn't want to tell him, how I happened to be asleep. "Oh, I'm here with Tamra too. So tell everyone she's ok."

"Are you ok?" he asked. "Cady, do you know where you are?"

"No, I know it's in a basement of some kind, but that's about it, Sorry." I said.

"It's ok babe, I will find you. I promise." he whispered.

Everything started to flicker, I must be starting to wake up, "Chase, I'm waking up."

He turned to look where I was talking, "No, not yet. I don't know where you are." He said worriedly.

"I don't know, but I'll figure it out and I'll try and find a way to tell you." I said.

Chase sat on the bed, and put his head in his hands, "I can't lose you, Cady. It would kill me, I love you so much," he said with tears in his eyes.

It started flickering more and more, I knew I had no more time. "I'll get out and I will find you, I love you," I said as I started to wake up…. …

I could hear the guy tied to the pole coughing, I woke up looking over at him, trying to focus. His hair, his body, oh my heavens, "Brad?!" I yelled. He looked up, and our eyes met.

He smiled, "Cady, is that you?"

I shook my head, "What are you doing here?"

He looked around, "I don't know. I went looking for you and someone hit the back of my head, and then I woke up here." Brad said.

"Hey, I'm here too!" Tamra yelled.

Brad whipped his head back to look at Tamra, "You must be Tamra," He looked back at me, "They are going to kill you both!" he said through gritted teeth.

I looked over at Brad, "Do you have any powers?"

Brad shook his head, "No, I think they shot me with something."

"Can we talk about this after we get our asses out of here, please," Tamra whined.

"How, when we don't have our powers back yet?" I said to Tamra.

"I think mine is coming back, I can feel it a little at least." Tamra said. I could smell the burning of the ropes. Please let her get them off before someone comes back.

I heard Tamra grunt and saw her hands come up. "You did it, Tamra!" I whispered loudly.

She came over to me, and undid my ropes and then we both went over to Brad. We untied his ropes, he and fell forward. I barely got him before he hit the floor. He struggled to his feet, trying to balance himself, saying, "I'm ok, let's just get the hell out of here."

We walked up to a door and heard people on the other side. I looked at Tamra and pointed to a large desk. We both went over to it, sliding it in front of the door. "Hopefully, that will hold them out for a minute or two," I whispered. We all started looking around the room to see if there was another way out.

It was a small room that had two chairs, a desk and a pole in the middle of the room. There were no windows that I could see. Brad went to the wall trying to feel for any type of window that might have been covered up. Tamra went in the middle of the room, holding her palms up and letting the fire fill the room with some light. It was just a flicker of light, but we used whatever worked.

I started looking at the ceiling for anything that might help. Great. Nothing up there, I looked for some time more and still nothing.

"Ok, I don't see anything on the ceiling. I'll check out the floor, maybe there will be something there." I said as I started looking at the floor. Hopefully, there will be a trap door of some kind around here.

I found a piece of carpet of the floor that looked like it had been cut. I messed with it enough to fold it over, and found a freaking trap door! "Oh, hell, yeah, guys get over here!" I whispered loudly.

Brad and Tamra both came running over, looking down. I opened the trap door and said, "I don't know where it leads to, but it's our best bet to get the hell out of here." Just then someone tried to open the door. Great, they'll be in here in no time. I looked over at Brad; and knew he had the same idea about them getting in here. "Brad, take Tamra and go, I'll hold them back." I told Brad.

"Are you freaking crazy, Cady? They'll kill you! I'm not leaving you." Brad said.

I had to do something, they'll be in here any second. "Brad, please go. Go find Bani, Chase they have help with they, but we all can't go. They will kill us all three, so please take Tamra, and get help."

Brad gave me a quick kiss on the cheek, "I will come back for you." I smiled and they jumped down, into the door.

I ran back towards the door, and on my way I grabbed the wooden chair I had been tied up to. I hid behind the door with the chair in my hand, and as Ian broke the door open and ran in, I swung the chair as hard as I could. The chair made contact with his head, and shattered the chair. I grabbed one of the broken pieces and rammed into his chest, saying, "How's that feel mother.....!"

Ian fell to the floor eyes wide in shock and fear. Then he started turning grey and shattered into pieces. That jerk better be dead. I grabbed the wooden piece and headed out the door.

I was in a long, nearly dark hallway with no doors that I could see. I ran to the end of the hallway, but it was a solid wall. "Shit, shit," I whispered in frustration.

I turned to go the other way, and I made to the end and found some stairs going up. As I headed up the stairs, I could hear people talking, so I stopped mid-way up and listened.

"Where the hell is Ian? I told him to go get that little bitch and bring her back here!" That voice belonged to

Vincent. I crept up a couple more steps, so I could hear the rest.

"Do you want me to go see what is taking him so long, sir?" the other guy asked.

"No, he's probably getting his fill of her first, the idiot," Vincent said. "Go make sure the room is ready for her. I want Cady to see everything that happens to her, before she dies. All my son had to do was get her blood and then get rid of that little Valkyrie, but he couldn't even do that right. But I can."

He said laughing. "What do you need her blood for, sir?" the man asked.

Vincent smiled saying, "With her blood, I can finally track down all the other Valkyrie. Now, after the room is ready, go get both of them." Vincent said. When did he take my blood? I wondered to myself.

"Yes, sir," the other man said. I could hear him shuffle his feet out of the room. I waited to see if I could hear Vincent leave, and after about ten minutes I could hear his phone ringing as he walked out of the room.

Talking on his phone, "Yes sweetheart, I'll be at Melzone's, after I'm done with….." Crap, he walked far enough away that I couldn't hear him anymore. I waited for a few minutes longer, and then opened the door. I considered running through the house and out the door, but as I looked around. I didn't have a clue where the door, that lead outside was.

I slowly walked down the hallway, staying as close to the wall as I could. I finally came to another door, and I slowly reached for the handle. I turned it gently, it started to open and stopped. I put my ear to the door so I could listen for anything or anyone inside. I didn't hear anything so I continued to open it and walked inside.

There was a closet and only one bed there with cuffs hanging off the headboard. In the center of the room underneath the bed, there was a hole in the floor."I wonder what that's for?" I thought to myself. "Oh great, this is probably where they were going to bring me and I brought myself. Good going, Cady." I thought to myself.

Twenty-Eight

One thing I noticed in this freaky house is that there are no windows. I haven't seen one yet, and that's just odd. I turned to go and a man was standing in the doorway. "Awe, I've been looking for you, Cady. Thank you, I would've hated to drag you fighting, all the way up here." he said. Then he smiled an ugly smile, "Are you going to be a good girl and get on the bed? That would make it even better."

"First of all dude, brush your teeth, they're gross. Second, why don't you get on the bed and show me exactly what I'm supposed to do." I said moving towards him. I looked into his eyes, and realized he was a demon.

"Bitch, just do as you're told and you won't get hurt." He said as moved towards me.

"Who the hell are you tryin to kid? You're gonna try to kill me." I said.

We were now about three feet from each other. He brought his hand up and shot out fire balls as he said, "Yes, you're right."

I dove to my left, hitting the floor. I rolled behind the bed, and tried to use my magic. Of course it's still wasn't working! Ok, time to kick his ass the old fashioned way.

I watched and waited for him to bring his hand back up to shoot at me again. When he did, I leapt up, and punched him in the face. He fell back, so I kicked him in the gut. That made him fly into the wall, and hit the back of his head hard, I watched as he slid down the wall. I ran up to him and grabbed his head, we fought back and forth. Until I finally got up on his head, grabbing and breaking his neck the way Chase had shown me.

"Great now what am I going to do with him?" I looked over at the bed and had an idea. I figured I would put him in the bed and make him look like me. I heard someone coming… shit, I have to move fast, so I started dragging his body to the bed. As I put him on the bed, I handcuffed his wrist to the headboard. Then I pulled the blanket until it was over his.

I ran over to the closet and got in, leaving the door cracked open. The door opened and Vincent stepped inside. "Cady, I'm sure you are just waiting to see what I have in store for you." Vincent chuckled.

"Mmm," I moaned, hoping he thought it was me under that blanket.

"Ian, must've done a number on you." he chuckled. "Well, I would love to stay and chat with you, but I have a date with my sweetheart." He put his finger up to his mouth. "You might know her. Her name is Mable." He snickered. "Oh, that's right she's your aunt," He laughed.

I can't believe he's dating Aunt Mable and she knows what he's going to do to me. How could she do this to me? I knew she didn't like me much, but damn. This is just plain mean of her!

"Have a great life, or what's left of it. I have everything I need from you, Cady. Your kind will make me more powerful than I ever dreamed of. Do you have any last words?" he asked. What the hell is he talking about? He waited to see if I would answer him, "No? Ok then, you have about five minutes to think about your life."

My heart was about to jump out of my chest. What if he decided to go over to the bed and look at me? Luckily he just stood at the door, and kept laughing.

"Are you ready to go?" Garrett said as he walked in. I can't believe Garrett is working with him too. Oh, this can't be good.

"Yes, I'm ready." Vincent said to Garrett. "Good thing Garrett told me about you Cady. A Valkyrie? I couldn't believe it when he told me, now with your blood, I can track down all the others and kill them too. Then no one could stop me. Goodbye, Cady." He said as he started throwing fireballs. Not at the bed, but under the bed. As he walked out, I looked over at the bed and saw lava coming up from the hole that was in the floor. Wow, he was powerful.

The lava was filling up fast and spreading everywhere. I had to get the hell out of there, now! I opened the closet door, and headed over to the main door. As I opened it up and ran out, I looked back toward the bedroom door. Lava was now coming through the door!

He was going to burn down whole place! Now I know where his son got his psychosis from.

I ran to another door, hoping like hell that this was the door that leads outside. When I tried to open the door, it was locked! Well shit, now what am I gonna do? I pushed on the door and nothing. I tried kicking the door open and again, nothing.

Behind me I heard someone yelling, "There's lava in the hallway! We gotta get the hell out of here!"

Then another voice yelled, "None of the doors will open! We need to go up!" Great, they were coming this way and it sounds like a lot of them. I kept kicking the door harder and harder, and finally it cracked at the edge. I kicked it again, just enough so I could get out. I squeezed out of the crack in the door, looked around and found a piece of wood. I placed the wood in front of the door, jamming it shut so no one else could get out.

I turned to look at the house, or what I thought was a house. It was actually a small mountain with a door. No wonder there were no windows. As I stood there, I could hear screams coming from inside the house. They were heading up the hill from the inside. They would be out in no time.

I turned to run down the mountain, and as I ran that I could hear the hissing of the lava coming down with me. I ran harder, and realized I was running down the mountain to an open field. I could see someone running towards me. Great, how did they get out and in front of me? As he got closer, I could start to make out who it was, and it was….Chase!

I ran and jumped into his arms, hugging him as tightly as he was hugging me.

"Chase, how did you know where to find me?" I said as I kept hugging him.

He cradled my face with his hands, kissing my lips, cheeks and neck, then back to my lips. "Your friend Tamra and Brad told me where you were." He mumbled through his kisses. I couldn't stop kissing him, and then he pulled his lips slightly back, "Babe, where's your shirt?"

"I kinda lost it," I shrugged.

He started laughing and took his shirt off and started putting it on me, "Here, wear this one."

"Chase, Garrett is working with Vincent, and he told them that I was a Valkyrie." I said as I put on the shirt.

"Son of a…." He said. I cut him off.

I turned around and said, "We have to go, now!" I could hear the hissing of the lava coming down the mountain,

Chase looked behind me, grabbed my hand and we started running. As we ran I noticed the flowers in the field, pink and black, the same flowers as in my dream. The lava, flowers, all were in my dreams.

All of a sudden, a truck raced passed us, skidding sideways in front of us. The truck stopped and Vincent jumped out, "Did you really think you could get away from me?" he asked.

"Well Vinnie, nice to see you again, and yeah I actually did," I smirked.

Chase put his arm in front of me. "You better get the hell out of our way, before I kill you," he growled.

Vincent just laughed, "You both can die together." He said as he shot fireballs out behind him. The trees burst into flames, so the fire was in front and beside us. His eyes turned blazing red as he threw fireballs at us, and we both dove out of the way. He threw some more at us as we both rolled out of the way.

Just then, I could feel the tingle in my eyes, yay! I thought my powers were coming back. I looked down at my hands, and electricity was dripping from my fingers.

I stood up, facing Vincent. He stared at me, smiling, "Good, are you going to stand there and let me kill you, like a real woman would?"

"Nope, I'm gonna kill you where you stand. Like a real woman should," I said smiling.

He went to shoot fireballs at me again, but this time I held my arm up, palm out to freeze the fire. There was a moment of shock on his face. He shot again, and again I froze them. I flicked my wrist and the truck went flying towards him. He dove out of the way, and as he stood back up, I had my chance.

This time I didn't wait for him to shoot at me again. I shot liquid ice at his chest. As it hit him, he started to freeze from his chest down. I smiled, "You demons think you're so powerful. Well, screw you, asshole."

I kept the liquid ice coming out. There was horror on his face as it started to freeze. When he was frozen solid, I stood there staring at him for a moment. I then brought my other hand up, and lightning bolts shot out towards him. He shattered into a million pieces.

Chase put his hand on my shoulders, I was shaking. "Babe, calm down, it's over." Chase whispered in my ear. I looked around and saw the lava still coming towards us and the fire was getting larger as it grew in front of us.

"Chase, I don't think we're gonna make it out of here." I said with tears in my eyes.

He turned me to face him, "I love you Catalina, I'll be right here with you the whole time." Chase brought his lips down to mine, kissing with passion and hunger. I kissed him back the same way.

"I love you. You are truly my dream guy." I said as I could feel the heat coming from the lava and fire over our bodies.

Twenty-Nine

The wind started blowing hard, and we look up to see the largest freaking tornado I had ever seen!

"Hey, can you two quit making out and help a sister out!" Bani yelled. I looked over at her, and she was standing on the far side of the lava. Tamra, Brad, Nate, Avan, Cooper, Violet, Brad and Oma were with her.

"What do you want me to do?" I yelled back.

She looked over at Oma and said something then looked back at me, "I'm gonna move the tornado around, and you use your liquid ice and aim it at the tornado! Oma is gonna do the same, it should start freezing the lava!" She yelled.

Bani started moving the tornado, and Oma and I both shot out liquid ice at it as it spun. The lava immediately started freezing. We stood there for what seemed like hours, but was probably minutes. I wasn't really sure, but my arm was starting to cramp up. When it was all said and done, all the lava had frozen and the fire had gone out.

Bani came running and grabbed me into a big hug. "I'm so happy, you're alive!" Bani shrieked.

"Me too, me too," Tamara said jumping up and down.

I laughed at both of them, "I'm fine, I'm fine. Thank you both for saving our butts."

Nate and Avan, came over and gave me a hug, "I'm glad you're ok, Cady,"

Avan said. I smiled at him, "Thanks, Avan."

Chase took ahold of my hand, and smiled, "Let's get out of here."

I squeezed his hand, "Sounds great to me."

We all loaded up in Oma's van, but Chase wouldn't let go of my hand. He looked over at me with a shy smile, "I thought I was going to lose you," he whispered.

I lightly kissed his lips, "That will never happen."

As we started to drive off Bani piped up and said, "Demons beware! Cady is here, and all mighty and powerful! You mess with her and her friends, and she'll beat some freakin ass!" We all just started laughing.

We pulled out of the field, when I looked back. "Oh my heavens! I thought we had killed him!" I yelled. Everyone looked back to where I was looking and there stood Vincent and Garrett!

All of a sudden they disappeared. "They'll be back. We need to prepare for that day. They'll bring an army with them the next time. We'll need a more powerful army." Oma said quietly.

"Oma, I thought...I thought I killed him." I said sadly.

Oma looked over at me and smiled, "He's a demon, my child. You will never know what kind of power he has up his sleeve, but he's gone for now and probably for a long while. We need to find out how he is going to use your blood. That is the main goal right now. As for Mable, she better be gone by the time we get back tomorrow." Oma said angrily.

We drove in silence after that, since everyone was exhausted. I think we all dozed off once or twice, but luckily Brad didn't he was the one driving

We decided to go back to Belton so Bani could get her stuff, and I could go through my belongings at my old house.

As we pulled up to my house, Bani looked at me with a sad smile. "Umm Cady?"

I looked back at and knew what she wanted. "Bani, you are staying the night, right?"

Her smile brightened up, "Well hell yeah, I am!" We said goodbye to Oma, Brad, Cooper, Violet and Tamra, since they were going back to Ballard. That way Bani and I could drive our cars.

Chase, Nate, Avan, Bani and I all went to the house. As we walked in, Chase grabbed my hand, "We'll get Vincent and Garrett, babe. I don't want you to worry."

I smiled, "I'm not goin to worry about it for a while. I just want to get through tonight and relax with you." I said as I kissed him lightly on the lips.

As I looked around my house, I noticed all the mail on the floor. "I guess since I've been gone, the mail still continues to pile up," I said laughing.

I picked up the mail and noticed a large envelope, when I opened it up, I gasped, and Chase came running over. "What's wrong?" he said worriedly.

I looked up at him. "It's from my...my mother." I said in whisper. I looked to see where the return address was from but it didn't have one. That in itself was odd. I pulled out the paper and started reading it with everyone looking over my shoulder.

Dear, Cady

If you are reading this, then happy 18st Birthday! I hope you had a good one. First, let me say that I'm sorry that I had to leave you, but things were happening that I couldn't explain to you. By now, I'm sure you are wondering what you are. You're not only a witch, but also a Valkyrie. I wish I was there and had an easier way to say it and to help you figure it all out. But that wasn't possible then, but since you are eighteen there is a way you can *come to see me. The amulet that I gave you is the*

way to this realm. I've left instructions on how to

get there. I will meet you once again.

I love you,

Mom

"You've got to be freaking kidding me……"

Don't miss "When the past comes back to bite" coming

soon.

www.ingramcontent.com/pod-product-compliance
Lightning Source LLC
Chambersburg PA
CBHW062020170626
46813CB00001B/232